Someone was stalking her, but who...and why?

While she sipped her water and slowed her breathing, she noticed a package by her front door. Puzzled, she went to inspect it. She wasn't expecting anything. It was a small bag with an envelope inside. It wasn't addressed or post marked, which she found odd, and she hadn't been here long enough to begin receiving any mail. Using her index finger, she sliced through the self-adhesive and pulled out the contents. It was a newspaper article and, when she turned it over, she realized it as from a local paper from Watertown where she had lived before.

The heading sent chills down her spine. It read:

Remembering the anniversary of the death of our local slain police officer Anderson Slade. A year later and the case still remains open.

After skimming the article and reading the details of the case, she saw that the end of the column stated the authorities claim the case was still being investigated and they would not stop until justice was served but they were no closer to bringing in a suspect.

Her hands shook, and she looked around the wooded area and across the pond. Seeing nothing amiss, she turned the bag upside down, searching for a clue as to who could have sent her this chilling message. For a moment, she even let her mind wonder if it was Andy speaking to her from the grave, urging her to remember that his killer was still at large. As if it were possible for her to ever forget. Kit shook her head to clear it and realized that thought was ludicrous and her imagination was getting carried away. Her attention shifted when she saw a small piece of paper flutter to the ground.

Kit Harwick has just experienced a tragedy that no one expects to go through. She thought she had all she ever wanted until her fiancé, Officer Anderson Slade, was murdered in cold blood, leaving her broken hearted. Forced to work through her grief and navigate life on her own, she decides to leave town and move closer to her grandmother, heading to the South and a new way of life. Her new neighbor, Rex Jennings, had to make the tough decision to leave his job on the New York City Fire Department to come back to a place where he swore he would never return. Trying to reinvent himself and reintegrate himself in his hometown, he wonders if this place has anything for him besides painful memories. He falls into a pattern of monotony until Kit moves in across the lake. The two of them could not be more different, and they find themselves at odds. Still, Rex would be happy to offer her all the "Southern Comforts," then Kit begins receiving messages from the past, reminding her that Andy's killer is still at large, and now he's after her...

KUDOS for *Southern Comfort*

In *Southern Comfort* by JD Davis, Kit Harwick's police officer fiancé has been murdered, so Kit moves to the South to be closer to her grandmother. Kit first meets her new neighbor, Rex Jennings, when he is skinny dipping with a woman in the lake. Kit thinks Rex is rude, uncouth, and amoral, but when she starts receiving mysterious messages from someone about her fiancé's murder, Rex is the one who steps up to help and protect her, making her feel safe again for the first time in a long time. That is, until whoever is leaving the messages tries to get up close and personal. Like Davis's other two books, this one is well written, fast paced, and the characters are marvelous. A really great read. ~ *Taylor Jones, The Review Team of Taylor Jones & Regan Murphy*

Southern Comfort by JD Davis is the story of a young woman whose fiancé, Officer Andy Slade, is murdered in cold blood. His killer is not caught, and a year later, Kit moves down South to a small town where her grandmother lives. She thinks it will be more peaceful and quiet than in the big city. And she's right, at first. Then someone begins leaving envelopes at her door—envelopes with reminders of Andy's murder. She feels threatened and turns to her neighbor, bartender and volunteer fireman, Rex Jennings. She doesn't really care for Rex and thinks he's a playboy, but he's there when she needs him. And need him, she will—if she wants to stay alive. *Southern Comfort* cleverly combines mystery, suspense, romance, and superb character development for a touching and poignant story that is hard to put down. ~ *Regan Murphy, The Review Team of Taylor Jones & Regan Murphy*

OTHER BOOKS
BY
JD DAVIS
AND
BLACK OPAL BOOKS

Judicial Justice

That's a Wrap

ACKNOWLEDGMENTS

Thank you to all who have supported my dreams. I appreciate it from the bottom of my heart and, as always, remember—if you can dream it, you can achieve it.

SOUTHERN COMFORT

JD DAVIS

A Black Opal Books Publication

DEDICATION

To my partner in crime and to TMZ, you are my favorite men and I am blessed to be your wife and mother. One day when you read this, I hope that you are proud, because I am so very proud of each of you. I love you and believe you can achieve anything you put your mind to.

PROLOGUE

The leaves crunched beneath his feet as he surveyed the situation before him. He had been at his post for hours, hidden under the town's water tower. From there he had a clear view of the police department and counted carefully the number of uniforms that had entered and exited the building.

It was important that he get this right. His life depended on it. If everything went according to his plan, justice would finally be served. He was going to take matters into his own hands, and he knew he had waited long enough. He had come out here every night for months and felt fairly competent that he had learned their routine.

He knew their schedule and knew that, at shift change, the officers would meet at the station. The daytime guys would relay the information from the calls of the day and the night time men would report for their duty.

He bided his time while the squad cars, one by one, retreated back to their homes, and through the well-lit office, he could see the two men left standing, refilling their coffee. Anxiety filled him, and he tried to school his breathing as beads of sweat rolled down his back beneath the black hoodie.

He checked his pockets for the extra rounds of ammo. The weight of the bullets calmed him as he rolled them around in his hand. If everything went according to plan, he would only need one. And if everything didn't go to plan, well, then he was going to be in much bigger trouble.

It was a risk he was willing to take. It was time this sleepy little town woke up. It was time they realized just who they had messed with. If they couldn't do their job, he would have to do it for them. He had waited long enough.

When one officer was left standing at the desk, he knew he had to act, or it would be a wasted opportunity.

He started forward, his eye on the prize. When he reached the foyer, he pulled his hood down over his face, careful to avoid revealing too much to the camera. He pushed the buzzer and saw the officer look up from his place behind the computer. He gripped his weapon firmly in his hand, and when the door opened, he raised his arm and fired.

The shot rang out, and the uniformed man wore a look of surprise and then one of fear before he gasped and grabbed his side. He never had time to retrieve his weapon and return fire before he hit the deck.

As much as he would have liked to revel in his accomplishment, he knew he needed to move. As the other officer came running to his friend's aide, the shooter's feet were already pounding the pavement.

The last thing he heard was the other man screaming into his radio. "Officer down. Shots fired. We need an ambulance."

When he got back to his vehicle he wasted no time firing up the engine and peeling away. He was only satisfied when the sound of sirens was headed in the opposite direction toward the station. When he was a safe distance away, he ripped off the mask and wiped the sweat from his brow. He couldn't believe he had actually done it, and the nerves set in. He had to work as he gripped the steering wheel to keep from shaking.

He looked at the picture on his dash. "That was for you. Now you will have justice."

෴

Kit was just about to switch off the light on the nightstand beside her bed as she set her alarm for the next day, when there was a knock on her door. The sound startled her.

It was an intentional hard knock that someone put some force behind as they beat against the wood. Before she could swing her legs over the side of the bed the doorbell rang.

Instantly she was alarmed. Who could be coming by at this time of night? She checked the bedside clock. Ten after eleven. What in the world? She grabbed her robe and hurried toward the door, and the bell rang out again, protruding through the silence of the rest of the house.

She could see the flashing red and blue lights blur through the window, lighting up the living room, and something inside of her told her that when she opened the door her life would never be the same. Her hands were cold and clammy, but she managed to get a grip on the door handle and forced herself to turn it.

On the other side of the door stood a face she had grown accustomed to seeing. The rookie that had been riding along with her fiancé for months stood wringing his hands. He wasted no time.

"Kit, it's Andy. He has been shot. I am so sorry, but

there is no time. We have to go. He has been air lifted to Mercy Medical. We've got to go now."

She felt dizzy. "No, it can't be. Is he?" She couldn't bring herself to ask the dreaded question.

"I don't know." He looked miserable. "Please, there is no time to waste. We must go."

Without looking back, she ran wildly to the squad car waiting to drive her to her worst nightmare. She was oblivious to the fact that she was wearing a night gown, housecoat, and slippers. To the officer's benefit he seemed unaware of her wardrobe as well.

They barely talked on the way to the hospital as the lights and sirens allowed them to blaze through every intersection and stoplight. The car had barely stopped in front of the emergency entrance when she hopped out and ran in to see Andy's brothers in blue gathered around grimly.

"Where is he?" she screamed wildly. "Someone please tell me where he is?"

The sergeant on duty grabbed her elbow. "He is in surgery, Kit. He lost a lot of blood. We are waiting to hear—"

"What happened? What happened to him?" she pleaded, waving her hands in exasperation and angst.

The officer looked down at his feet. "He was ambushed. Never saw it coming."

"How could this happen?" she cried.

Just then a surgeon came out to meet them. Exhaustion was etched on his face, and his scrubs were stained with blood. Her stomach lurched in to her throat and her heart leapt from her chest.

"Is Officer Slade's family here?" he asked.

The sergeant responded. "We're all his family, but this is his fiancé, Kit Harwick. How's he doing?"

The doctor shook his head sadly. "Hello. I'm Dr.

Witten." He paused. "I'm sorry. We did everything we could. His injuries were too significant. I'm sad to say he didn't make it."

Kit didn't remember what happened next. She just knew that everything went hazy, and she could no longer stand. After she fell onto her knees, her screams echoed through the building.

CHAPTER 1

I think that is the last of it, Ms. Harwick," the moving man stated as he hefted the last box inside.

"Thank you, Joe," she said as she looked at his name tag once again and dug into her wallet, looking for a tip.

The man deserved more than what he had charged her after all the hard work he and his crew had put in. Moving was hard work and unpacking it all would prove to be just as tedious as loading all of her belongs had been.

"Thank you, ma'am, but really it isn't necessary. Your grandmother already took care of the bill."

He looked at her sympathetically. She knew that look all too well. He knew about her heartbreak. That was part of the reason she had had to leave. She couldn't exist in a world where she was constantly being given sad puppy dog eyes and whispered about before she was even out of earshot.

They would talk in hushed tones. "That's the girl I was telling you about. Her fiancé was murdered in cold blood."

No, she hated being pitied and, although people meant well, she could never move on in the small rural community of Watertown. There were too many reminders of what her future could have been like, should have been like. There were too many sympathetic stares for the fiancée of the slain Officer Anderson Slade. Not to mention the unsettling fact that they had never caught the man responsible. A killer was still on the loose. How could she walk the streets and ever feel the same?

She couldn't go to the grocery store or stay out after dark, much less find sleep in the bed that was to be the same one they shared as a married couple while there was a dangerous man out there.

A year later and they were still no closer to finding the man responsible for ruining her life.

"Taking a trip down memory lane dear?" her grandmother, Mellie, asked her.

"I was just thinking of how much work I have ahead of me. That's all."

"Give yourself time. It will all come together."

"Right. I hope so."

"The ladies of this family are strong and so are you. This is a fresh start, Kit. You will see."

Kit smiled at the wrinkled woman beside her. Strong was an understatement. She hoped she could find that inner strength in herself someday.

"Just put one foot in front of the other, and before you know it, you will be getting somewhere. Are you sure you don't just want to stay with me? My house is awfully big and there is room enough for the both of us."

"I appreciate the offer, but the cottage is fine. You have done enough. If I'm going to make a life for myself here, sooner or later I'm going to need to learn to live on my own again."

"I suppose I understand your way of thinking, but I

just want you to have the right mind set. The south is a different way of living. Promise me, you'll keep an open mind."

"I promised before I moved to Middle Bay that I would be accepting to change and I intend to keep my promise. You act as if I didn't come from a small town and that I have never been accustomed to the rural quaintness and quirkiness that can come with it."

"Yes, but living in the Midwest suburbs is a bit different than the southern hospitality. I just want you to see its charm and possibilities."

"I am not afraid of disliking country traditions as much as I am of not fitting in."

"Oh, poppycock. The people of Middle Bay will love you. Just watch out for alligators and stock up on mosquito repellant, and you will be just fine."

"I'll try and stay out of the swamp, Grandma. Now, my biggest fear is tackling these boxes."

"You will get to it when you get to it. It's the southern way. Now, I'll fix us some tea. Do you prefer sweetened or unsweetened?"

"Sweetened, I suppose, is the correct answer."

"See. You're learning already. A little sugar and hydration will bring some color back into those cheeks. Sweet girl, if I am being perfectly honest with you, you look absolutely skeletal and peaked. Some Arkansas sun and a good meal is just what you need."

Kit doubted that vitamin D was going to cure her blues from all of her misfortune, but at this point, she was willing to give anything a try, including ice tea drinking and front porch sitting.

The cicadas hummed and the humidity left the air soggy and heavy. A breeze that was ever so slight pushed through the branches of the weeping willow that overtook the whole right side of the front yard. The branches swayed and danced in the wind, leaving her entranced at the simple beauty of nature.

Suddenly, laughter broke into her thoughts and a shrill woman's squeal drew her attention away from the tranquility of the afternoon. Kit stood and, after a moment, followed the sound of the screams. She hustled down the walkway and pushed some of the low hanging branches out of her line of vision, ducking her head as she went. Holding the handrail, she tentatively stepped down onto the narrow wood dock.

Laughter rang out in the midst of all the splashing.

"Rex, stop. Give me back my clothes. Oh, you are truly wretched, aren't you?" a female voice said with a laugh.

"Come out and get them," the male teased.

Kit felt like she was intruding but couldn't help herself. She leaned forward, positioning herself around a hanging limb. She nearly gasped out loud when she saw the man was completely naked. The woman had ditched her clothes and was skinny dipping in the small pond. The man held her clothes teasingly trying to beckon her out of the mossy water. She squealed and protested a little too loudly, but her tone and body language said she was secretly delighted.

Kit watched the exchange of the strange mating call while admiring the man's muscular back and toned buttocks. His body was a sight to behold, and she shifted her weight to her other foot causing a stick to crack loudly. "Shit, shit, shit," she whispered, hoping it went unnoticed.

No such luck. The man whirled around in a full monty.

Kit's eyebrows shot up and, against her will, she glanced down before looking away as quickly as she could.

"I—I'm sorry," she stammered. "I didn't know anyone was down here," she lied.

Out of the corner of her eye she could see him smirk.

"No harm done," he said easily.

"Okay, well then. I'll be leaving." She turned and scurried up the stairs.

She could hear him chuckling behind her and couldn't resist turning around.

He had covered his groin with a Hanes T-shirt that had long since been white. His grin was wide and cocky as he lifted his hand in a small wave.

She turned and continued running back to her cottage where her grandmother waited with the tea.

"Do you know that a man and a woman are skinny dipping in your pond in broad day light?"

Her grandmother barely looked surprised. "I see you've met your neighbor, Rex Jennings."

CHAPTER 2

Who's the female he was with?"

Mellie pursed her lips in mock disdain. "That would be the flavor of the week. It's always a new one tramping through here. I couldn't keep them straight so I just as well quit trying."

"If it bothers you, then why do you let him continue to rent from you?"

Mellie's face softened. "While I may not agree with all of Mr. Jennings life choices, he is a sweet boy. He just has a wild streak that needs to be tamed, that's all."

Kit wouldn't have used the term boy to describe him. That insinuated a pubescent teenager. No, she had gotten an eyeful, to her dismay, and he was all man.

"A wild streak," Kit mused. "He is not a little mischievous boy, Mellie. From the looks of it, he is all grown up, although I can't say the same for his maturity."

The older woman's eyes held a twinkle. "I see you're getting you color back. I can't say I'm surprised at that blush on your cheeks. He's a handsome one and tends to have a way with the ladies. Although, I urge you to be careful and I must say those are some pretty big assumptions for such a quick first impression."

"I don't need to be mindful because I have no intentions of socializing with your tenant, although neighbors we may be. If you say he is nice enough, then it must be true, but I know his kind. He's egocentric, inappropriate, and unapologetic for his lack of manners. Typically, that is not the kind of person that I associate myself with."

A knowing smile played on Mellie's lips.

"Why are you smiling at me like that?"

"Maybe because she knows you would be absolutely mortified if the person you were talking about happened by and overheard just what you thought about him."

Kit froze, said a string of curse words in her mind, and gave Mellie her best thanks-for-nothing look. She slowly turned around to face the intruder and inevitable introduction. When she was forced to make eye contact, Kit winced apologetically. "Do you always sneak up on other people's private conversations?"

He crossed his arms over his chest. "Do you always make assumptions about people that you know nothing about?"

She stuttered. "Well, I—

"Relax. No explanation necessary. I may not be the best at first impressions, but I've got a way of growing on people." He flashed that megawatt grin. "Eventually, you won't be able to help yourself."

"Oh is that right?" The tone in her voice was enough to indicate that she highly doubted that.

"Yes, as a matter of fact. You might even find me irresistible."

She snorted. "I find that highly unlikely, but in the event, that happens, I promise to do my best."

The duo shared a staring match, both too stubborn to look away from the silent challenge.

"Oh, you two act like you have known each other for

years. I told Kit that she would fit in here."

"Yes, I feel the warm acceptance already," Kit said sarcastically.

"Not with that attitude," Rex said pleasantly enough. "But I can give you a real warm acceptance if you like."

He raised his eyebrows at her in invitation.

"You have got to be kidding me. The sheets haven't had time to cool since the last one, much less wash them, and you've known me all of five minutes. Does that act actually work for you?"

"Trust me, it's taken less time than that, and who says we made it to the bedroom."

Kit rolled her eyes. "Oh for Pete's sake."

"On that note, my work here is done. Welcome to Middle Bay. I'm sure I'll be seeing you around the bend in the crick," he drawled and indicated his small cottage on the other side of the pond.

She nodded her head. "Neighbors."

"Don't hesitate. If you need anything at all. A cup of sugar." He grinned. "As long as you realize I don't actually don't have any, but you get the point."

"Thank you." The words came out of her mouth, but her expression read that she would not look for ridiculous reasons to make her way over to his house on a lonely night.

His expression brightened and turned mischievous as if to say challenge accepted. He turned his attention to Mellie. "Ma'am." He nodded his head in respect. "Sorry for the interruption. You all enjoy your day."

He strutted down the front porch stoop with his Wranglers hugging his hips and curving over his rear just right. The way he carried himself, walking tall, shoulders back, told her that he knew it too.

"Mmmhmm," Mellie said smacking her lips.

Kit looked at her in surprise.

"I may be old, sweetheart, but I'm not dead. He's one good-looking man."

"He may be okay to look at, but men like that, men with a wild streak as you call it, they don't need to be encouraged."

"That part may be true, but I really think if you give this place a chance, you might be able to fill that void and be happy. Are you excited for your teaching job? Apple of Our Eye is a very prestigious school, especially for our area, for early childhood development. They seem very excited to have you join their team, and I just know all the littles are going to love you. Kit, what is wrong?"

"I'm just nervous, Mellie. Everything is changing. And that's what I thought I wanted, you know. I wanted to move on, to move away from all of the heartache. Start fresh. As it turns out, it seems to have just followed me here. I moved out of our house, I'll be starting a new job, I don't know anyone or anything about this place. New beginnings are supposed to be exciting and full of possibilities.

When Andy was alive, I loved a good challenge and felt like I could tackle any obstacle. Now instead of feeling happy flutters of anticipation, I'm wrought with knots of anxiety. Instead of feeling nervous excitement, I'm terrified. I'm petrified of starting over alone. There's nothing familiar here to remind me of him, and that's what I thought I wanted, what I thought I needed, but now I'm scared I am going to lose pieces of him. What if I forget what it was like to walk hand in hand down the sidewalk or if I can't remember what it was like to swap plates half way through our meal at our favorite restaurant, or the smell of his aftershave, the sound of his voice going on duty over the radio, or the feel of him sliding into bed after a night shift when I have already been asleep for hours. I'm just scared."

Her voice was trembling beyond her control. "I'm defined as a widow, but I never got the privilege of calling him my husband. I'm lost and have to start over, and I'm not sure how to do that. There's no manual on how to pick up the pieces of my broken, messy life." Kit threw her face into her hands.

"Kit, baby." Mellie walked over to her and began to rub her back in the kind of comforting way that only grandmothers can do. "I wish I could tell you exactly what to do and exactly how long it's going to take until you start to feel better, but unfortunately it doesn't work that way. Grief has a way of taking over. It was like I was drowning in the sea and couldn't breathe. The waves overlapped each other, and there wasn't a life preserver. And then, eventually, there was a break in the waves, and I could tread water in between, but the grief was not any less daunting when it washed over me."

"And now?" Kit asked.

"I've been washed back to shore, and I've found my footing, although the waves still come, I have learned how to become a stronger swimmer, but I would be lying if I pretended that sometimes a storm would not come along and the sand would wash out from under me, knocking me on my ass. Sometimes the little waves can take you by surprise and make you lose your footing, but you will find it again. It feels like this horrible tragedy defines you, but it will get better and life will be worth living. Not all at once, but slowly, and you may not notice when it happens, but you will smile again. Truly smile, because something is funny and you can't help yourself.

"You owe it to yourself to live, and you owe it to Andy too. He's with you, and he wants you to be happy, until you can meet again. One day at a time, one moment at a time, and sometimes what you accomplish on a day is merely surviving, but you will get there, and we are all pulling for you, because we love you so much."

Kit dabbed her eyes. "Thank you, Mellie. I am trying. I'm going to really try. How are you so strong?"

"Unfortunately, it comes from life experience, dear. You're strong, too, and when you can see clearly again, you will be even stronger."

The women embraced.

"I hope so." Kit sniffed. "I really hope so."

CHAPTER 3

The shrill ringing of the alarm clock roused Kit from a deep sleep. She had finally reached her REM cycle only a couple of hours prior. Nerves had kept her awake most of the night and, even when sleep had claimed her, she tossed and turned restlessly.

Kit rubbed her grainy eyes and reluctantly forced her bare feet to make contact with the chilly hardwood floor as she searched idly for her house slippers. Andy had always made fun of her for wearing the beat up ratty-looking moccasins, but they were a go-to comfort rather than a luxury.

She stretched to work out the kinks in her tired body. She was used to functioning on such a little amount of sleep. Many nights were spent worrying, nursing an aching heart, and lonely.

Mellie's words came back to her. One foot in front of the other.

"Push through, Kit. Don't let the enemy win. You can do this."

Suddenly, she decided that what she needed to do was put those words to work, literally. Kit glanced at the clock and knew that there was plenty of time. She laced up her Nikes and dug out her ear buds that she plugged into her phone.

She stepped outside, took a deep breath, and hit play on the familiar play list from her running days. The music filled her ears, and she put one foot in front of the other as her feet began to move across the gravel road.

The roads were new, but the old routine came back to her as she knew how much distance she had covered based on what song was playing. A sweat worked itself across her body, and she focused on breathing in and out. The rhythm and fluid movement came back as if she had never stopped.

The repetitive motion was therapeutic, and it was the lightest she had felt since that fateful night. The night everything changed. The night Andy was taken from the earth forever. She started to breath faster, and tears blurred her vision as memories came flooding over her.

The harder she cried, the harder she ran. Her lungs burned as she gulped in the crisp autumn morning air. She was going to run this heartache out if it was the las thing she did. It had to get better from here. Tears flowed freely, and she could barely see her surroundings, but she didn't bother wiping them away. Somehow the release felt good.

It was like the dam had burst and opened the flood gates, relieving all of the pressure that had built up inside of her. She was a ticking time bomb, and it had only been a matter of time before she blew.

"Son of a bitch."

The car screeched to a halt. The smell of burnt rubber penetrated the air, tarnishing the clean country air as it assaulted her nostrils.

The driver quickly turned off the rock music that blared so loudly she could hear it over her own music playing through her headphones. She was so close that she could feel the vibrations of the bass coming off of the hood of the vehicle. Kit looked down and realized the driver had come mere inches from swiping her legs out from underneath her.

"Are you okay?" the man asked quickly, as he hopped out from behind the steering wheel.

"I'm okay," she replied breathlessly, pulling the ear buds out of her lobes, quickly wiping her tear streaked face, and blotting her eyes to clear her vision.

She must look a site, she thought. When she moved her hands away from her face, she was dismayed to see Rex Jennings standing with his hands on his hips.

"What the hell is wrong with you? You practically ran right out in front of me. I nearly clipped you. You could have seriously been taken out."

She bristled underneath his words and, between his chastising tone and aggravated stance, his entire demeanor pissed her off.

"I must not have heard you coming over my music." She indicated her phone. "But I'm not sure how I did not hear you, given the sheer volume in which your radio was blaring. I'm sure that did not prove to be a distraction at all, and the speed at which you were traveling is not really conducive to this curvy gravel country road. I think it's safe to say we were both at fault here. I've learned my lesson if you've learned yours."

He stared at her in astonishment.

"What are you looking at me like that for?"

"Are you always this feisty?"

Now it is her turn to put a hand on her hip. "I am not feisty."

"Okay, my mistake. Argumentative."

"I am not argumentative."

He gave her a look to indicate that she was in fact arguing about not arguing.

"Ugh. Why must you try to frustrate me?"

He smiled. "Do I get under your skin?"

"You say that like it is a good thing. Trust me. It is not."

"That's what you say now." He maintained his Cheshire grin.

"Well, as stimulating as this conversation has been, I cannot be late for my first day of work, so I've got to be going. I'm sorry I wasn't paying attention and nearly ran out in front of you."

"Well, look at that. She can apologize, and you almost sounded genuinely sincere."

She rolled her eyes in mock distain.

"In all seriousness though, are you sure you're okay? You look as though you've been crying."

She turned her face away in embarrassment. "What? No. I had something in my eye. It's chilly out here, and it made my eyes water."

Rex looked at her for a moment before accepting her answer. "All right then. Do you need a ride home to make sure you make it to work on time?"

"No, it won't take me that long to make it back. Besides, I think we might be bad luck for each other. It's probably best if we steer clear of each other," she joked with mild humor.

He harrumphed. "Just being neighborly. Wouldn't want the teacher to be late on her first day of school."

Her head snapped toward him. "How did you know that I'm a teacher?"

"Relax there, teach. Small town. People talk."

She let out a sigh.

"Don't worry you will get used to it," Rex stated as he got back into his car.

"I sure hope so," she muttered as she started back toward her house.

Feeling somewhat embarrassed, she jogged the path back toward her house. While she sipped her water and slowed her breathing, she noticed a package by her front door. Puzzled, she went to inspect it. She wasn't expecting anything. It was a small bag with an envelope inside. It wasn't addressed or post marked, which she found odd, and she hadn't been here long enough to begin receiving any mail.

Using her index finger, she sliced through the self-adhesive and pulled out the contents. It was a newspaper article and, when she turned it over, she realized it as from a local paper from Watertown where she had lived before.

The heading sent chills down her spine. It read:

Remembering the anniversary of the death of our local slain police officer Anderson Slade. A year later and the case still remains open.

After skimming the article and reading the details of the case, she saw that the end of the column stated the authorities claim the case was still being investigated and they would not stop until justice was served but they were no closer to bringing in a suspect.

Her hands shook, and she looked around the wooded area and across the pond. Seeing nothing amiss, she turned the bag upside down, searching for a clue as to who could have sent her this chilling message. For a moment, she even let her mind wonder if it was Andy speaking to her from the grave, urging her to remember that his killer was still at large. As if it were possible for her to ever forget. Kit shook her head to clear it and realized that thought was ludicrous and her imagination was getting carried away. Her attention shifted when she saw a small piece of paper flutter to the ground.

She knelt slowly to pick it up and realized that the glossy texture was a small piece of a photograph. She had to focus to see what it was a picture of. It appeared to be a triangular cut out, but of what? She squinted. Was it a blue backpack?

She flipped it over and over in her hand to figure out the significance of the picture although her gut said it wasn't placed in the bag by accident, but what was the meaning behind it?

She stood there long enough that the sweat had dried and a cold chill had replaced the dampness. She looked at her watch and realized she was running out of time to get ready for work.

"Pull yourself together, Kit. You've got kids to teach."

అఎఎ

Kit picked at her fingernail polish while she waited outside of the director's office. She watched as parents walked their children through the front door and to their classrooms. Some of the moms wore sweatpants, carrying a baby on their hip, flustered and stained, sleep deprived, but totally in love with their little humans they were raising.

Other moms came rushing in, their heels clicking across the linoleum foyer, seeing their children to school before heading off to their careers. Most of them were doing their best to keep it all together, and all of them expected their children to be in good hands while they were gone.

They were entrusting the school with the most precious thing in their life—their children. It was a job that Kit did not take lightly.

As Kit was lost in thought, the director came out to greet her.

"Hello, you must be Kit. I am Kari Schneider."

"Hello. It is nice to finally meet you, and I appreciate you conducting most of our business and interviews over the phone. It meant the world to me while I was deciding whether to move here or not."

"It's nice to meet you as well. We're excited to have you. You class room is overcrowded and really a big job for one teacher. I know that she will be extremely grateful for the extra hand. We were pleased to learn that you have training in not only early childhood development, but also experience with learning disabilities and behavioral issues as well. We have some kiddos who could really benefit from your expertise to better prepare them for kindergarten," Kari said, her voice bubbly and charismatic.

She was a petite woman who used a lot of hand movements to express her enthusiasm, and Kit couldn't help but find her energy contagious.

It had been a long time since she had felt animated about something, and focusing on her profession might be just what she needed.

"I haven't had much time to explore your little town yet, but so far I find it quite charming, and I am looking forward to meeting my class. I may have needed this change as much as you needed the extra set of hands, so thank you for giving me the job."

"Around here everybody knows everybody, so when Mellie said her granddaughter was the perfect person for the job, her recommendation carried a lot of weight and held value to me. We all just love her here."

"That warms my heart, and I'm glad to be with family," Kit said sincerely.

"I must say Mellie spoke so highly of you that I was surprised we hadn't met until now. Did you ever come to visit?"

"As a young child, I vaguely remember coming here for some short visits during the summer, but I'm ashamed to say it was she that did most of the traveling to see us. It has been a decade and a half at least since I have been here. She moved back here for good after my grandfather left."

"Yes, she doesn't speak of it much. Word had it that he passed some time ago."

"That would be correct. My parents were never what I would call very family oriented. I regret that they were not more accepting." Kit shrugged sadly. "They were more self-absorbed; I suppose you could say."

"We cannot pick where or who we come from unfortunately," Kari said softly. "But no reason you should carry their burden."

"Yeah, I suppose," Kit mused. "I look forward to making up for their short comings, and I've enjoyed developing a relationship with her. In many ways, she is my only real family."

"Well, she's a good one to have." Kari smiled. "Look, Kit, your grandmother informed me of the tragedy you have been through and told me that you're looking for a fresh start. I'm not trying to bring it up, but I want you to know that I am sorry for the tragic loss of your fiancé, and around here we can never have too many friends. So, if you need anything at all, don't hesitate to ask. We're family, and it's a tragic state that our country is in, cops not feeling safe to do their jobs, but we like to think we live in a one of a kind bubble here. Neighbors are still neighborly, and we may be a sleepy little place, but you're safe here, and we want you to feel welcome."

Kit squeezed her hand. "Thank you, I appreciate that. It will be nice to feel safe again." She thought back to the message that was left on her doorstep that morning and hoped that there was truth behind what Kari said. "I could use a change of pace," she added.

"Things are slow around here. Most of the working people commute to the next town, but if I can get used to it, anyone can. The quaintness grows on you."

"I look forward to it."

"Good, are you ready to meet your classroom?"

"Yes, of course."

"Great. One last thing." Kari hesitated. "I have to ask you something."

"Uh oh, what is it?"

"We have had some guest visitors come in to do an occupational presentation to the class, to talk about their jobs and such."

"Okay, I bet the kids love that."

"Yes, but I feel awkward bringing this up on your first day, but I feel you should have a fair and proper warning."

Dread suddenly filled Kit. "Why do you say that?"

"Today's presenter is one of our local police officers."

CHAPTER 4

Although the morning went smoothly, Kit watched the clock, knowing that by early afternoon, today's occupational presentation was revolving around law enforcement. That was her luck. She respected all first responders, but on her first day, it couldn't have been any other professional besides a police officer. She put a smile on her face and promised Kari that she could handle it.

He walked in at precisely two-thirty, looking polished, professional, and friendly. He was dark haired, light eyed, broad shouldered, and dimpled. Her heart gave a little leap when he smiled in her direction.

She blushed instantly, foolishly assuming he was aware of what was going on inside of her.

Mary Jane snickered. "I wasn't sure which officer they would send, but I can't say that I am disappointed to see that it's Brady Renshaw. Our next half hour just got a whole lot more enjoyable."

Kit gave a small smile. MJ was a bubbly effervescent woman with a calm voice and kind eyes. She epitomized the stereotypical characteristics of a kindergarten teacher.

The kids buzzed with anticipation when they saw the man in uniform, and the handsome officer more than obliged their excitement.

"I will gladly answer all of your questions, just let me talk to your teacher first." He looked up and met her eyes. "I don't believe we've met."

"No, we haven't. I'm new."

"Today is her first day. She's our new teacher," a little boy responded helpfully.

"Does the new teacher have a name?" he asked kindly.

"Oh, of course." She laughed. "My name is Kit Harwick. You must be Officer Renshaw."

"Yes, I hope my name is all that has preceded me."

She smiled. "Yes, that's the only information I have."

"Good. Call me Brady." He shook her hand, and his warm one engulfed her petite cold one.

She only hoped that it wasn't clammy as well, and that he didn't' sense her nerves.

"Okay, Officer Brady. We have a room full of kids that are very excited to hear you speak. Is everyone ready to hear about what a police officer does?"

The room exploded with children's chatter.

"I'll take that as a yes. If everyone can calm down, we can begin." Kit moved her hands in a motion to indicate quiet.

The children immediately fidgeted in their seats, but got quiet so that they could hear what the policeman had to say.

"Hello, everyone. I think that I know most of you, or your parents at least, but for those of you who don't know me, I'm Officer Brady Renshaw. I have been serving this town as a police officer for over nine years. My job is to protect the people of Middle Bay."

For the next twenty minutes, the officer gave a detailed description of what his job entailed in easy to understand terms for a youngster. He left out any scary tales and described his position as a person who was there to help and that the kids should always feel comfortable talking to him. When he concluded his speech, the floor was opened up for questions.

Everyone's hands shot up into the air.

"Well, I would say you have attracted more little fans than the school nurse," MJ said. "Okay, kids, one at a time. Ryan, you first."

"Have you ever taken anyone to jail?" Ryan smiled triumphantly, confident that his question was the most well thought out.

Brady smiled. "Yes, unfortunately, I have, but only because sometimes even grownups need a time out to think about their actions. Usually, they do better after we're able to talk to them."

"Do you drive around with your lights and sirens on?" another kid asked.

"Only when going to emergency situations that we need to get to fast. It's a way to let people know we're coming to help them and so that other people won't get in our way and slow us down. Good question. Next."

"Do you have to take a test to become a policeman?"

"Yes, we do, and the test is to make sure we know all the rules and are strong and physically capable of helping people. If you study hard, you can be a police officer too."

"Have you ever shot someone?" a child's voice called out from the back.

The room got silent as some of the kids considered the possibility for the first time.

Kit felt uneasy and avoided looking at Brady's face.

"I have never shot anyone, no."

"But you have a gun," the kid persisted.

"That's right, I do, and I have been trained on how and when to use it and how to be safe. No one should ever handle a gun unless they have had proper training. We have a gun to protect ourselves and other people, but we never use it unless we have to, and we all have to stay up to date on our training. Thankfully, most of us never have to use them."

Kit felt a sickening feeling in the pit of her stomach and braced herself for what the child would ask next.

The boy seemed satisfied with Brady's answer. "My dad has a gun. It's bigger than yours, but he only shoots deer. I'm not allowed to go near it, and he keeps it locked in a safe unless he's hunting."

"That's right. People who go hunting also have to have proper training and special permits on when they can use it. You should never go near a gun without adult supervision and always tell an adult if you have access to a gun or if someone talks about a gun. It's important to always be safe so that accidents don't happen and no one gets hurt."

Another kid tentatively raised his hand. "Do bad people have guns?"

Brady looked over at the teachers, searching for advice on how to answer to their maturity level. Kit felt like someone had sucker punched her, and she grabbed the corner of the desk to steady herself.

"That's nothing you need to worry about, Teddy. Middle Bay is one of the safest places on earth and has some of the best people living in it. That being said, police officers are here to help you and protect you so if you ever do get scared about anything at all, you can come talk to us and we will help you. We took a vow to make sure this town and everyone in it stays happy and safe."

Kit let out a sigh of relief at his very appropriate answer. "Well, kids, that's all of the time we have for to-day. Let's all give Officer Renshaw a big round of ap-plause for taking time out of his busy schedule to come talk to us."

The room suddenly became boisterous as the chil-dren smacked their hands together clapping, banged their chairs against their desks as they pushed them back in, and scattered to their cubbies for their backpacks.

"Before you line up, Officer Renshaw has some honorary badge stickers to hand out so make sure you get one."

Brady tried to make eye contact, but with all of the children swarming him, he was distracted, and she avoid-ed it like the plaque.

"Are you okay," MJ asked her sincerely.

"Yes." Kit sighed. "Just overwhelmed. I assume you know about my past?"

"Yes, a couple of us were informed just in case you needed some extra understanding."

"Thanks, I appreciate that."

"Is there anything I can do for you?"

"Actually, will you thank Officer Renshaw for the both of us and excuse me while I go to the restroom. I'm fine, really. I just think I've had enough excitement for my first day." Kit grabbed her purse and hurried for the door.

೧೨೦೧

MJ knocked on the door of the bathroom stall tenta-tively. "Kit, are you okay?"

"Yes, I'm okay." Kit sniffed. "Thanks for checking."

"No problem. I don't mean to pry, but you don't sound okay. Are you sure?"

Kit unlatched the door to the stall and reluctantly came out dragging her feet.

"Was it the questions asked of Brady that upset you?"

Kit shook her head and leaned her forearms against the sink. "No, it's not just that. I think I'm going to love teaching here at Apple of Our Eye. The kids are great and they just want to learn. Of course, they're going to be curious about a policeman's gun. What inquisitive four and five-year-old wouldn't be? However, bad men do have guns. A bad man, with a gun, shot Andy and is still running free. Luckily, Brady answered the question wonderfully. Hopefully, no nightmares will be reported by the parents' tomorrow. The real reason I think I'm on edge even more than usual is that it's coming up on the year anniversary of the shooting."

"That must be even harder than usual. I'm so sorry, Kit."

"I'll be better tomorrow, hopefully not such a mess."

"You weren't a mess at all, Kit. You were great, and the kids really took to you, but you're not just going to go home and be by yourself in a new place. You have a friend now. You're coming with me."

"That's really kind of you, MJ, but I'm not really sure if I'm up for it."

"I'm not taking no for an answer."

Kit laughed. "Well, then what are we going to do?"

MJ clapped and gave a little hop in delight at Kit's acceptance. "First, we're going to my yogalatis class. You'll love it, trust me. It's a great way to decompress."

Kit raised her eyebrows. "And then?"

"And then, we're going to get a drink. And before you beg me off, which I can see in your face is what you want to do, let me ask, what do you have better to do?"

Kit bit the corner of her lip. "Besides, unpacking a million boxes, I guess I see your point."

"Great, and you have your whole life to unpack, but you'll never get another today."

Kit couldn't help, but visibly relax. "You know, you're good at this, talking me out of a dark hole and peer pressure and all of that."

MJ shrugged. "What are friends for?"

❧❧❧

"That was amazing. I feel so loose and relaxed. Do I look relaxed?" Kit exaggerated.

"You could probably benefit from a few more sessions, but meditation and the mind-body connection is very healing, but so is alcohol."

Kit laughed. "So where are we going to get that adult beverage?"

"Let's see, the options are limitless. We should probably choose the only establishment in town."

Kit's eyes widened. "You guys only have one bar in town?"

"Middy's is only one major one where most of the normal town folk are patrons. The other one is a hole in the wall, smells a little funky, and the patrons are of a one of a kind, sometimes rather odd variety. So for your first outing, we really only have one choice."

"Middy's it is. Do we need to change first?"

"No, trust me, it's uniquely casual, especially during the work week."

"Perfect."

"Come on, it's up here around the corner."

"I love that everything is in walking distance in Middle Bay. It's so convenient."

Music poured from the open door, and the aroma of fried food filled their nostrils, threatening to discredit the calories burned during their workout.

"This place is hopping," Kit exclaimed over the crowd. "I'm impressed. It looks like the entire population of the town is piled in here."

"Remember when I said there wasn't any other places to choose from? That may have something to do with it. Besides it's thirsty Thursday, which means half-priced burgers, a pitcher of beer, and wing special. Trust me, the wings are smoked, smothered, and then fried. They don't disappoint. Pair that with a frosty mug of ice cold beer and a cheddar bacon burger, and it's enough to bring out the farmers, teachers, construction workers, and preachers."

"Sounds amazing and I'm starving."

"Watch out," MJ shouted in alarm as a male arm reached out and pulled Kit toward him. Her face was buried in his soft flannel shirt, and she was caught off guard as a dart whizzed past her head, lighting up the score board when it connected with the dart board.

"Are you okay?" the hard-bodied male asked her.

Kit looked up, pushing away from his chiseled chest. She had to lean back to peer into the stranger's face because he was a whole foot taller than she was. "You?" she said, surprised.

"Me," he said, smiling down at her.

She pulled the rest of the way out of his grasp. "What are you doing here?" she asked, befuddled.

"Let's see, what am I doing here? I work here."

"You're a bartender?"

"Try not to hide your surprise or judgmental stare." He leaned in and whispered in her ear, "It's not polite."

The hot breath against her skin and such close proximity sent goosebumps down her body and a pang in her lower belly that was almost foreign.

It had been so long since she had felt the raw pull.

"I didn't mean to insinuate anything by it. I only meant that there's only one bar and restaurant in town so, of course, you would work at it."

"Yes, well, I guess I can see how that would be a disappointment to you. In order to fit into our little community or to have any kind of social life, you'll have to run into your attractive, charismatic neighbor. I could see how that could be such a calamity for you to have to deal with." His voice dripped with sarcasm.

"Such an impressive vocabulary you have, but are you sure you didn't mean to say acrimonious and cantankerous instead?" Her words carried a biting tone, although her wry smile revealed that she was teasing.

"Me, difficult?" he said innocently, raising his eyebrows. "I just saved you from a dart puncturing your temple, or worse, losing an eye. You should be thanking me that you don't have permanent brain damage or that your vision is still intact, but you're insulting my education level and my witty personality."

She stood with her hands on her hips, shaking her head, a smile playing on the corner of her lips, try as she might to contain it.

"Is that a smile I see, Ms. Kit all serious, no fun and games Harwick?"

"You're so dramatic."

"I thought you chicks dug that."

"You're so chauvinistic."

"You love it."

"And presumptuous and sexist. For the record, I'm not that surprised that you're a bartender. Now will you kindly get me a drink, some annoying man is grating on my nerves and I'm extremely parched."

"Fine, but I'm am charging you double."

"It should be on your tab. You did almost hit me with your car this morning."

He stared her in the eye. "Now is that any way to be? I thought we moved past that? All right, all right, one drink at regular price," he relented. "But I'll need to see some sort of ID."

"Seriously?" She gave him an exasperated look. "Bless your heart," she said, mildly sarcastic.

"Yes, states law says we have to card anyone forty-five or younger, even if they look right at that cut off."

She swatted his hand. "You really are deplorable."

He smiled, revealing perfectly straight teeth with the exception of one slightly turned in bicuspid. The crooked tooth did nothing to detract from his pearl whites and, in this case, actually added a little character to his lazy grin. His dimple deepened, and his smile reached his eyes and held the stare a moment too long before moving on to the attractive blonde on the next barstool over.

MJ gave her a knowing look.

"What?" Kit asked.

"I see you've met the resident hottie, Rex Jennings."

Kit shrugged and tried to appear indifferent.

"Oh come on. You can't say that he isn't good look-ing, and he's just across the pond from you. It would be convenient."

"Convenient, maybe, but I'm not interested. He's not the type of person I would normally give a second look."

MJ gave her another knowing look and smiled as she took a long swig of her beer. "He obviously doesn't feel the same."

Try as she might, Kit fought to not look over in the bartender's direction, but curiosity won out and, when it did, she was greeted with the site of Rex engaged in conversation with another customer but his eyes were on her. He winked at her in a cheeky response.

"Deplorable. The man's deplorable, I tell you."

MJ took another sip of her drink. "And hot, don't forget hot."

CHAPTER 5

MJ pulled up to Kit's house. "So, I'll see you tomorrow bright and early."

"Thank you again for inviting, or should I say forcing me to go out tonight? I actually had a pretty good time."

"Well, good. I'm glad. I foresee us having many more nights like this in our future."

Kit smiled graciously. "It feels good to have someone I can call a friend."

"I know what it feels like to be the new girl. Now, don't forget to take some Ibuprofen and drinks a lot of water. The kids show no mercy the day following thirsty Thursdays."

"Dually noted. Thanks."

Kit got out of the car and heard a voice that was becoming familiar. "You ladies having a slumber party? If so, don't forget to put my name down on the invite list." Rex wiggled his eyebrows suggestively.

"What are you doing here?" Kit asked, ignoring his obvious innuendo.

He smiled mischievously. "Just making sure my new neighbor made it home okay. I wasn't sure if you could handle your alcohol."

"I can handle myself just fine," she responded, annoyed. "I'll see you tomorrow, MJ." She closed the door and walked up the stairs to her cottage.

MJ laughed to herself as she pulled away.

Kit sighed in frustration as she dug around in her purse.

"What? Can't find your keys?"

"I'm sure they're in here somewhere." She knelt down and began pulling out every item. When the purse was empty, she shook it upside down in disbelief.

"Come on, admit you do not have your keys."

"Someone must have taken them." Kit shook her head anxiously. "It's the only explanation."

"Of course, that's the only explanation, jump to the most dramatic and pessimistic conclusion. It tends to fit your MO. Is it plausible that perhaps you just misplaced them?"

"No," she said, panicked. "No, that's impossible."

"Ah, I see. It's impossible that you could make a mistake." He rolled his eyes and rocked back on his heels. "Well, since you seem to have everything under control, I guess I'll be going."

Rex started walking back toward his lighted cabin across the lake.

Once the silence ensued, she was aware of the darkness and the eerie quiet. The thought of being left outside in the uncharted territory was enough to make her swallow her pride. "Wait, you do not understand," she called out.

"You're right, I don't. For someone who obviously needs help, you can't admit you may have made a mistake, and you definitely can't ask for assistance."

"I know that's how it seems, but I did not misplace my keys. I know that I didn't because—" She hesitated. "—because I'm kind of neurotic about thinks like that."

Rex snorted sarcastically. "You, neurotic? I would have never guessed."

Kit looked at him pointedly. "Seriously. When it comes to knowing where my keys are, locking my doors, looking over my shoulder, knowing where all the exits are in a public place, and generally just being paranoid, I'm somewhat of professional."

"Is it some kind of obsessive compulsive disorder?"

"No." She wrung her hands. "It's fear."

Rex could see the honesty of her statement. Her nervous fidgeting and softened facial expression almost pleaded with him to stay and help her, although it was almost against her own will.

He started back toward her. "What are you afraid of?" he asked curiously.

"I would rather not talk about it." Her voice shook with emotion so he just stood next to her on the porch, nodding as if he understood, even though he had no clue. "Let's just say, I'm obsessed with feeling safe," she continued. "And after this morning's cryptic message, and now my keys are gone—"

"What message? Are you okay? Is someone messing with you, Kit? You can tell me."

She shook her head and tried to brush it off. "I'm sure I'm just being silly and melodramatic. This is the South, right? You can trust people here."

"Whatever you aren't telling me has obviously affected you more than you're are willing to admit. You're shaking." Rex reached out and rubbed his hands over her arms and she flinched at the contact. "Hey, relax," he whispered. "I'm not going to hurt you. It's going to be okay."

She allowed herself to be wrapped into his arms, and for a moment, feeling his strong grasp and being pressed against his hard able body made her feel protected, allowed to be vulnerable, and shielded from life's injustices.

Kit nearly imagined his compassionate embrace was sincere and not completely self-serving. In an attempt to captivate her with his softer, nurturing side in order to arouse her senses that had been dulled by alcohol.

She jerked away abruptly. "Look, I would appreciate your help, but that's all I need. I just need your help getting back into my house, and if we could hurry it up a little, it's cold out here."

"There's that demanding, entitled, self-righteous attitude. I was afraid I had lost you."

She shot him a snotty look.

"You have two options at this time of night."

"What is that?" she asked.

"You can call Mellie and ask her for an extra key or you can stay at my place, and we can get the key tomorrow."

"Seriously? That is the best you've got? I cannot call Mellie at this time of night. What would I possibly say? Hey, Grams, I just stumbled in from the bar and somehow lost my keys to the cabin I rent from you. Don't worry, I'm just standing outside in the cold with a strange man that I have already seen naked when he went skinny dipping with some giggling blonde chick."

"It does have a certain ring to it. I'm sure she would understand." He laughed. Then his voice changed. "You think about me naked?" he asked gruffly.

She felt a tug in her belly, but she immediately denied it, shaking her head no. "No, of course not, but how could I forget the first time meeting my intolerable neighbor, he was engaging in sexual indecencies right out in my back yard, and he has been a pain in the ass, every encounter since."

"You're so judgmental." He clicked his tongue

against his teeth. "Besides, I'm not trying to be a black mark on your virtue. I wouldn't want to be the reason you can't wear white on your wedding day. You can marry your beloved with your dignity still intact, although if you change your mind, I promise it would be a good time."

Kit recoiled as if she had been slapped. "What did you just say?"

Her face must have shown her horror.

"Relax, Kit, it was just a joke. You know, something people usually laugh at. You have heard one before?"

Kit's hands were visibly trembling when she picked up her purse, and it had nothing to do with the drop in temperature. "I think you've done enough. I'll figure it out on my own." Her voice shook with emotion.

She started down the stairs with no destination in mind, but needing to move. It was not far into town. She would just walk to the motel, to get a few hours of sleep before she had to go to work. All the bed and breakfasts would certainly be closed down for the night. She knew she should not have let her guard down. What had she been thinking? Andy had always taught her to be aware of her surroundings, and here she was locked out of her home. It had not even been a week, and she was in an entirely unfamiliar area, a completely different state. She would really look like an imbecile now.

"Kit, wait. Where are you going?"

"To get a room."

"Now, that's ridiculous. I told you, you can stay at my place."

"Thank you, but no," she said while still walking.

"Okay, look, whatever I said obviously upset you. Kit, will you just stop? I cannot in good conscious just let you walk in the dark cold night by yourself. No matter what we think of each other."

She continued on her journey despite his pleas.

"Dammit," he cursed. He jumped down the steps and chased after her. "Damn blockheaded woman." He grabbed her arm and pulled her to a halt. "Will you just stop already and listen?"

"Get your hands off of me," she yelled.

"I will when you quit being so stubborn and listen to my proposal."

She didn't answer him but instead lifted her chin defiantly.

When he knew he had her attention, he exclaimed, "Are you always so hard headed? You can't even accept help. You're so irritating."

She yanked her arm from his grip and looked away, tears shining bright in her eyes.

"Now you're going to cry. Shit." He threw his hands up in frustration. "How is it that you are capable of making me feel like a heathen, even when I'm trying to do the right thing? I'm not this big bad wolf after the innocent sheep."

Her lips trembled as a big fat salty tear rolled into the corner of her mouth. She brushed it away furiously, mad at herself for letting her emotions get the best of her and with a witness being this man, nonetheless. When she found her voice, she finally said, "Are you going to tell me the options or stand there and insult me further."

"I'm not an expert locksmith by any means, but I'm willing to give it a try. If I can't get you into your house, I will drive you to the motel myself. I have a couch, but seeing that that is not an option, we can go with the first two choices. What do you say?"

He met her eyes, and she nodded her head in agreement.

"Okay then. I will just get my tools out of my truck."

Kit nodded again and assumed the position of waiting on the stairs. She pulled her arms inside of her shirt sleeves and tugged the thin material over her knees, rubbing them vigorously, trying to stay warm.

She remained silent as Rex worked on picking the lock. She did not dare turn around for fear of jinxing any positive outcome. She said a prayer in her head.

"You know, you should chip away some of that hard exterior if you want to fit in here. It'll make the transition that much smoother for you."

"Thanks for the advice," she grumbled.

"Can I ask, why did you move here anyway?"

"You can ask, but it's way too long of an answer." She cradled her face into her hands. "How's it coming?"

"You can turn around now."

When she did, he was smiling triumphantly and her door was standing open.

"You got it." She jumped up, relieved. "How did you do that?"

"I'm good with my hands."

Kit rolled her eyes. "Well, regardless, thank you so much. It might have been a little rough, but I do appreciate your help. Even if your opinion is not too high of me. I cannot wait to get bundled up under the covers." She stood in the doorway. "I owe you one."

He smiled and stepped a little closer. "I can think of a few ways you can repay the favor."

She met his gaze. "You're impossible, but even so, thank you."

"You're not as tough as you pretend to be," Rex whispered quietly. "I think I know what can melt some of the cold front you put on."

"Rex, I thought we established that we're obviously polar opposites."

"Yeah, yeah, I'm the charming bad boy out to ravage the pristine ice queen. I get it."

"I'm not an ice queen," she countered. She sighed with exhausted frustration. "Haven't we argued enough for one evening? Thank you for saving the day, but we can't get through two sentences without disagreeing."

"Some people would call that chemistry."

"Some people would be wrong."

"Rex," a female voice called across the pond. "What are you doing? You told me to meet you here and I've been waiting forever," she whined.

"Shit," Rex muttered under his breath.

Kit closed the screen door and was about to close the heavy wood one as well. "Deplorable, yes, my first assumption was correct. Absolutely deplorable."

"Kit, it's not what you're thinking."

"Really? Because I'm thinking you were trying to proposition me while you already had a girl keeping your bed warm."

"Rex, if you don't hurry, I'm going to have to finish by myself."

Rex winced.

"Classy," Kit said, raising her eyebrows.

"Okay, maybe, it *is* kind of as bad as it looks."

"Well, lucky for you, it doesn't matter much, thanks again for your help. You better go, she's waiting."

With that, Kit closed the door and left Rex standing on the porch in the dark.

e/oe/o

Rex rolled over and hit the alarm clock, groaning with annoyance. His hand knocked over the watered down glass of jack he had sitting on the night stand.

"Oh, dammit," he sputtered.

His pounding head told him that Jack was an asshole

last night. He opened the top drawer and felt around until he found the bottle of pain killers. He circled the cap until the arrows lined up and then used his thumb to pop the top and shook out two more pills than the recommended dose. He needed to shake the headache and clear his fuzzy memory of the night before.

He tossed the pills in the back of his throat and swallowed hard. He started to roll over and stopped short when he saw a smooth naked leg poking out from between the covers.

His eyes followed the curve of the female body and saw the blonde hair sparkling out from the other side of the pillow.

Rex braced himself on his elbow and tried to cautiously lean over the top of the woman's body to get a look at her face without waking her.

Lisa, damn, she was a hard one to get rid of. He shook his head as if to silently chastise himself for his poor decisions. He really needed to evaluate the parade of the blondes that he had thrown into a late night rotation. It required very little effort on his part, but more and more the next morning, instead of waking up satisfied and satiated, he woke feeling restless and grouchy. It was not the women's fault, but their neediness and predictability had begun to grow old and started to grate on his nerves.

He stepped into the shower and let the spray wash away the stench of alcohol and the remnants of shameful emotionless, drunken, passionless sex. As the water ebbed away and eventually dulled the jackhammers that had been going full force on his brain, memories from the night before came flooding back: Kit's face staring back at him—panicked when she was fearful, saddened and angered when he had offended her, relieved that he was able to help her, and finally disgust at his player reputation and his poor taste in which he displayed it.

The last look was what had driven him to drink. The way she was surprised to hear Lisa's voice calling out for him then resigned, and had he imagined disappointment? Whatever look it was made him feel dirty, inadequate, like he should be ashamed of himself.

Who did she think she was? Ms. High and Mighty did not deserve to look down her nose at him while standing on a pedestal. Just then, female hands reached around him and naked breasts were pressed against his back.

"You're up earlier than usual."

"I've got some things I need to do today."

"I hope the first thing on your to do list is me." She nipped his ear harder than what would be considered pleasurable.

The move made him want to swat her away like an annoying insect buzzing in his ear.

It was not fair. She did not deserve that kind of treatment, and he knew it, but he was already hung over. What did she want from him?

"As nice as this all is, I really do have to get moving. Would you be a doll and put on some coffee?"

"Struggling this morning?" She laughed. "Did somebody have a little too much fun last night?" she asked in a sing-song voice that made him want to shove his head through the wall.

"You know it," he lied. "Now, please, make me some coffee."

"Sure thing, Mr. Jennings, but you owe me one." She gave him a firm groping before stepping out of the steam-filled shower.

Rex breathed a sigh of relief when she was gone. What was wrong with him? A beautiful woman tried to seduce him in the shower, and he could not wait to get rid of her.

"Get it together, Jennings," he said to himself.

When he was dressed and felt somewhat human again, he came out of the bedroom. Lisa was waiting for him in her bra and panties with a hot steaming mug.

"Thanks," he said, taking it from her.

"Last night was great," she said huskily.

To keep form replying, he took a big drink and the hot liquid scalded his tongue and burned all the way down. "Mmm," he mumbled. "You can let yourself out. I've got to run. Thanks for making the coffee."

"Okay."

The disappointment was obvious on her face, but to keep himself from feeling guilty, he pretended not to notice. "I'm sure I'll catch up with you soon," he said as he started out the door.

"You don't have to wait until you see me at the bar, you know? You can call me."

"I'll do that," he replied, knowing as soon as the words were out of his mouth that he had no intentions of doing any such thing. If she were smart, she would know he was lying too.

He hopped in his pickup and drove the familiar roads until he pulled into the parking lot of the preschool. Checking his watch, he flipped the visor to look in the mirror, making sure his eyes were not too bloodshot.

It would have to do, he thought as he entered the building.

The director greeted him. "Hello, Mr. Jennings. Welcome to Apple of Our Eye Preschool. The kids are excited for you to be here."

I'm sure they're the only ones, he thought wryly. "Please, call me Rex."

"Of course, well, Rex, right this way. The class is ready for you."

CHAPTER 6

When Rex walked into the classroom, the kids were playing at their centers. He knew the moment she saw him that she had not been aware that he was the guest speaker of the day. Surprise was visible on her face.

"What are you doing here?" she asked.

"I'm the guest speaker for occupations."

Her mouth opened, but it took a moment for her to speak. "But why?" she managed. "You're a—"

"A bartender?" he finished. "I'm also a volunteer fire fighter."

Shock registered again.

"That's right, teach. You don't know everything."

She pursued her lips, and when she had gathered her thoughts, she said, "Well, neither do you, Mr. Smarty Pants. I'll round up the kids."

"Mr. Smarty Pants? Wow, you have a foul mouth, teach. Are we resorting to playground insults?"

"In my classroom, I'll not tolerate vulgar language so I can't exactly be a bad example and say what I'm really thinking."

"Understood. Do as I say, not as I do. It's the way of the world, right?"

"I try to do right in the world as well, Mr. Jennings, but sometimes certain situations make it near impossible. Nevertheless, these kids are looking forward to a firefighter speaking. Keep in mind, in their eyes, you're a hero."

"And what am I in your eyes?" he asked, his tone changing.

"It doesn't matter what I think. It only matters that they receive a message that inspires them."

"I've got it. I'll try to keep the bad language to a minimum."

She gave him a look that said he better not even think about using his extensive vocabulary.

"I'm not a monster, Kit, geez."

"I never said you were," she said quietly.

"Yeah, well, you didn't have to. Your eyes say plenty."

She shifted her gaze to MJ and indicated they were ready to start. "Okay, class, take your seats. We're ready to hear from our very special guest, a fire fighter, Mr. Rex Jennings."

The whole class cheered and rushed to their desks. They sat on the edge of their seats and gave him their undivided attention.

"Hello, all. As your teachers have said, I'm Rex Jennings, and I'm a fire fighter here in Middle Bay. In this town, we do not have a full time department because we're so small, so instead, it's on a volunteer basis. Luckily, we do not get that many fires, but before being employed by our town, I was a lieutenant for the New York City Fire Department. It's one of the largest fire and rescue teams in our country, and I worked alongside of some of the best fire fighters in the nation."

Kit swallowed hard against the lump in her throat, and it could only be what she thought was pride.

"Now, when you think of fire fighters, everyone thinks of the obvious, that we're predominately fighting fires, right? We also respond to other emergent situations like car accidents or other natural disasters. We're trained in first aide, and I got a degree in fire safety and EMS, which stands for emergency medical services. So we were all also emergency medical technicians, otherwise known as EMTs, so that we can provide full service help to anyone in need."

Kit listened as intently as her students and had to admit Rex was right about one thing. She did not know everything, and she as more than a little shocked and impressed by his credentials. Just because she was wrong about him professionally did not mean that she was wrong to judge him personally, right? His social life was obviously a mess, and his personality was one of the most frustrating she had ever come across.

When she looked back up at him, she noticed that the room had grown silent.

"Oh, I'm sorry. Class, if anyone has questions for Mr. Jennings, now is the time."

Hands shot up around the room, and she called on them one by one.

"Do you have to go to school to be a fire fighter?"

"Yes, I have a degree in fire science and obtained a certified first responder with defibrillation certificate. Most departments also require you to be an emergency medical technician so I am also a licensed paramedic."

"How strong do you have to be?"

Rex laughed. "Well, I like to think you have to be pretty strong. In all truth, you have to stay physically fit in order to do the job to the best of your abilities."

"How hot do fires get?"

"There are a lot of variables...er...things to consider, but the average fire is one thousand, one hundred degrees Fahrenheit. In other words, very hot, but we wear fire resistant clothing so we're able to go into a building to save people."

"Have you ever been scared?"

"I'd be lying if I said I've never been scared or been in some tough situations. There have been a few close calls, but that's why we stay up to date with our training and you have to trust the guys you're working with. A little fear is good. It keeps you on your toes and more aware of your surroundings."

Kit stared at him in awe.

"Why did you stop fighting fires in New York?"

Kit watched Rex's face change, and he chose his words carefully.

"I just needed a change of pace. This town is slower and is where I was born and raised. I guess it just made sense to come back here eventually."

Kit did not believe his answer for a second. It just did not make sense to leave his career as lieutenant of one of the most competitive and sought-after jobs in the country. The waiting list alone was enough to scare most people away from attempting to apply for such a prestigious and honorable position. No, something was not right, and there was definitely more to the story, but she had to remind herself that it was none of her business.

He did not have to talk about it, and she should not even care. Why would she? The man was undeniably intriguing. All the more reason she should stay away.

"Okay, kids, last question."

"If you are all volunteers here, what if nobody volunteers to go to go to the fire? People will get hurt and there will be no one there to help them."

Rex glanced over at her and she was reminded of

how Brady had done the same thing the day before when one of the other kids asked if bad people had guns.

She tried to coax him with her eyes to try to deflect any negative questions. The kids did not need to be traumatized by irrational or even grown-up rational fears. It was not for them to worry about.

"You never have to worry about that, Tommy. All of us are dedicated to helping people, but I personally promise you that I will always show up. Even if nobody else can make it, I will show up, but you do not need to worry about that. Everyone in this town helps everyone."

The boy visibly relaxed as did Kit.

"Okay, everyone, please give a big round of applause to our special guest speaker Mr. Rex Jennings."

The kids clapped rambunctiously and, when the bell rang, they dispersed to the coat racks for recess.

"Special, huh?" Rex questioned her.

"What?" she asked, confused. "Oh, brother. I say that about all of the guest speakers. Don't flatter yourself."

"Wasn't yesterday your first day?"

"Yes, so?" she answered, mildly annoyed.

"So who was your special guest speaker yesterday?"

"Officer Brady Renshaw."

Kit could not mistake the dark look that clouded Rex's face like a sudden rainstorm that came on with no warning.

"What? Was it something I said?" she asked, genuinely curious.

"No, no, it's fine. Officer Brady Renshaw is certainly always known as a special one."

"Yes, he is," he agreed.

"You would think that," he said snidely.

"Uh oh, two hometown heroes at odds. What's

wrong? Is it guns versus hoses with you and Officer Renshaw?"

"Nothing that you would understand so it's best to leave it alone."

"Fair enough. It's none of my business. On the other hand, you did a good job with the kids today. I was pleasantly surprised, and I believe they were all impressed."

He met her eyes and held her gaze intently. To her own frustration, she was the first to look away.

"I must admit I was shocked. I did not expect that about you. It was a wild card considering..." She hesitated and tried to find the right words. "...I just mean with all of your training, education, and prior experience and you still..." Her cheeks grew slightly pink with discomfort.

"And I work at a bar. It is okay, you can say it. I told you, teach, you do not know everything."

She licked her lips and fidgeted. "Well, I better get going to help the lunch supervisor."

"I will let you run away in a second, but first I wanted to say something. Something I said, upset you last night."

She waved him off. "Too much to drink, I suppose."

"I do not think so," he countered and met her eye.

"Let's just say, you do not know everything either and leave it at that."

"Fair enough." He raised his hands in surrender. "In your words, it's none of my business."

For a moment neither of them moved.

"I really need to help MJ. The kids can be unruly if they're hangry and not being served fast enough."

"All right, I'm sure I'll see you around Ms. Harwick."

"It seems to be unavoidable." She smiled. "And I

reckon we'll exchange not-so-pleasant pleasantries and friendly banter in the near future."

She gave her best impression of a Southern accent. Rex shook his head. "I look forward to it."

ഇഇഇ

"So what was all that about?" MJ asked her.

"All what about?"

"The weird sexual tension between you and Rex."

"There was not," Kit exclaimed, outraged.

"I beg to differ. You could cut it with a knife. All that arguing, brooding, and pensive staring are the recipe for chemistry. He's our local bad boy that every lady wishes to tame, but he remains a wild mystery."

"Well, I'm not looking for a wild mystery or a bad boy. In fact I'm not looking at all."

"He's not a real bad boy. He's like one of those re-formed men—a good man with a little bit of a wild streak. You know, the right choice but all the wrong reasons. The right combination of completely vulgar and lewd meets sexy. Just enough to entice good girls to go to the dark side."

Kit looked at her with fascination. "Wow, you have really given this a lot of thought. I hate to burst your incredibly imaginative bubble, but I find Rex to be infuriating the majority of the time. However, nevertheless, he was an asset to me last night after you dropped me off."

"Oh yeah? An asset in what way?" MJ leaned in with anticipation for all the sordid details.

"Not like that." Kit swatted her arm. "Come on, now. What kind of girl do you take me for?" Exasperation filled her voice.

"Human, I suppose, although I'm beginning to question that. Anyway, go on. You did not get neighborly with your neighbor."

"No, but I was locked out of my house and could not find my keys anywhere. I know I had them. I double check those sorts of things, and I have made a habit of always paying attention to detail ever since..." Kit paused. "Well, you know."

MJ turned serious and nodded her head in understanding.

"Admittedly, I was on the verge of hysteria when I could not find them and, of course, my logical conclusion was that someone must have stolen them, which, of course, Rex thought was absolutely absurd. We then got in a somewhat heated debate about my obsessive need to be right and my inability to just say please and thank you when asking for help. Apparently, I'm not quite well adjusted to the Southern way of things, but nevertheless, he was able to somehow pick the lock so that I wouldn't have to call my grandmother and make a nuisance of myself at such a late hour or get a room at a bed and breakfast, which saying it now, sounds more ridiculous, but after his innuendos, there was no way I was going to accept his invitation to stay at his place."

"He offered to let you stay at his place?"

"Yes, and get this. Another girl from the bar was already occupying his bed and, judging by his surprise, he had forgotten he already had a guest."

"I'm sorry I missed this," MJ exclaimed. "Who was she?"

"I do not know. Does it matter? I get the feeling his place has a revolving door and there's no shortage of occupants going in and out."

"You could have called me."

"I know, but I did not want to bother you, but I was going to ask if by chance I left them in your car?"

"I do not believe so, but I can check."

"Thank you. Mellie is dropping off a spare set, but it makes me paranoid to know that the original set is out there. I know it may sound silly thinking someone would want to get in my house, but after the weird message I received the other day, I'm just a little on edge."

"After everything you have been through, it's understandable why you would feel leery, although I highly doubt it's anything to worry about—" MJ stopped. "Wait, what message?"

"Someone left a bag on my porch yesterday morning. I found it when I got back from my run and after yet another exchange with the charming Mr. Jennings when he almost hit me with his car. As far as I could tell, it was not sent by mail, but instead hand delivered. In it was a newspaper article, rehashing details of Andy's murder for the year anniversary and reaching out for people to come forward if they have any details."

MJ's eyebrows shot up. "What? Why would someone do that?"

"Maybe to let me know they were not giving up on solving the case, maybe to keep me informed since I'm no longer in the area, but Andy's coworkers are good for keeping me in the loop. I guess what struck me as most odd was if someone's intentions were of a helpful nature, why did they not leave a note or explain they were thinking of me? Instead I felt kind of ambushed and a little uneasy. I'm sure I'm over analyzing, but when I could not find my keys on top of it, unsettled became unglued."

"Rightfully so. I'm sorry I left without making sure that you made it in safely. I just thought with Rex there…" MJ trailed off.

"You just thought you were excusing yourself in case we had spontaneous romance." Kit smiled wryly. "I know. It's not your fault, but Rex got me in my cabin, and he returned home to the lady of the night to keep him company. All turned out fine, but to answer your question there, absolutely nothing going on with Rex Jennings and me, tension or otherwise."

MJ smiled. "Whatever you say."

CHAPTER 7

As promised, the shiny metal was waiting for her. It stuck a little as she tried to turn the knob as new keys had a tendency to do. She put her weight behind it and jiggled anxiously.

"Having trouble?" a voice asked her.

Was he everywhere?

"No, just a new key," she answered, exasperation evident in her tone.

"Okay, I just thought it looked like you could use a little bit of help."

She turned on her heel to face him. "You don't always need to be my knight in shining armor, you know. I'm perfectly capable of handling things on my own."

"It looks like it," he said sarcastically.

Did he always have to have that smartass look on his face?

"What are you doing here?"

"I saw you come home and just wanted to check on you. Forgive me for trying to be polite."

"You, polite? I'm not sure those two things belong in the same sentence."

"Probably not," he agreed. "Look, we may not have

gotten off to the best start." He continued up the porch stairs. "May I?" He indicated the stuck key.

She stepped back to allow him space. "Go ahead."

He jiggled in much the same way she had, and she started to roll her eyes, but just then the door popped open.

Lucky bastard.

"How did you do that?"

He smiled a cocky smile. "Wouldn't you like to know?"

She put her hands on her hips.

"You just have to make sure it's aligned correctly. Hold the handle still as you do it, otherwise, it's a little loose and it misses the mark."

"Ah, well, thank you." She started to proceed through the door.

"Wait, are you going to grab your package?"

Her eyes whipped around to the bag that was sitting on her porch swing. It was identical to the one she had received previously. She began to sweat, even in the breezy temps.

"I guess I didn't see it there. Thank you." She tried to appear relaxed and hide her nerves.

"Special delivery?" he asked.

"Maybe something like that."

"What's wrong? You look like you've seen a ghost?"

"Why does something always have to be wrong?"

"You tell me, Ms. Harwick. You look like an eight-day clock all wound up and shit. I'm still trying to figure you out. What's your story?"

"Don't bother trying to figure me out. And I don't have a story. Just a lot of boxes to unpack."

"If you say so." He rolled back on his heels. "Well, I really just wanted to say that we've not had the best introduction. Maybe we could start over, seeing as how we are neighbors and all."

She eyed him cautiously. "Sure. We can call a do over."

She seriously doubted they could move past the opinions already formed of one another, but for the sake of another argument, she might as well appear to occasionally be agreeable.

"Well, it's settled then. I'll see you around, Ms. Harwick."

"Rex, you can call me Kit." She gave her best attempt at a friendly smile.

He tipped his imaginary hat in reference to a Southern gentlemen.

She was pretty sure he had not been a Southern gentlemen a day in his life.

She watched him walk away and started to reach into the bag. She pulled out a laminated newspaper article and immediately recognized the heading. It was dated from almost a year ago.

Before reading it she dug deeper and felt a glossy shape of a small piece of paper. Another cut out of a photo.

"Rex," she yelled.

"Yes?"

"Will you come back here and—" She wet her lips. "Do you think you could just do a walkthrough of my house?"

Without hesitation he made his way back quietly. "Are you sure that everything's okay?" He looked skeptical.

"Y—Yes," she stammered. "I mean probably. Just precaution. Please."

His eyes searched hers, asking questions without words. "Okay, sure thing, Kit."

Her stomach gave a flutter at the way he put emphasis on using her first name.

"But, Kit? I have to tell you, it's becoming apparent you're lying about not having a story, and I'm a sucker for a good mystery."

"I wish I could say the same," she murmured as she followed him into the house.

✅✅✅

"Are you sure this was not just a ploy to get me inside of your house so you could tie me up and use as your own personal pleasure slave?"

"You're disgusting. You know that? So much for starting over with a clean slate."

Rex stepped around another set of boxes and flipped on the lights in the next room. "Who says neighbors can't have friendly conversations, or relations for that matter."

"Friendly yes, relations no."

"Does any of this have to do with the package that you received?"

"Why would you think that?" she asked abruptly.

"Because that's when you started acting all weird on me again. What was in it anyway?"

"None of your business."

"Oh, I see. Probably some secret boyfriend you left behind somewhere."

"Not quite," she replied.

Just articles about the most important man to me that was murdered, and I have no idea why or who is sending them. So much for moving on in a place where the past could not haunt me, she thought.

"So did you leave anyone behind? Or are you trying to make the long-distance relationship thing work?"

"Wow, cowboy, you're about as subtle as predicting a chance of showers in the middle of a hurricane."

"So are you going to answer me or just keep me guessing?"

She smirked. "I thought you liked a good mystery."

"I do, but only ones that I can start to figure out." He stepped forward, closing some space between them.

Pride kept her from stepping back, but they both knew that she wanted to.

"You're cute when you tease."

A blush crept up through her cheeks. She turned away quickly.

"Shall we check the next room? If an intruder was here, they would have had time to get away by now," she huffed.

"There's that demanding sarcasm. Let's go, mystery girl."

"I hope your house guest was not too mad last night. I'm sure you were able to charm your way out of trouble, though—a quality that must come in handy often when in situations like those."

"Ouch, that was quite a burn. Okay, it was a dirty move, but I truly forgot she was coming over. Honest mistake."

"Different girl than the one in the lake?"

"Wait a minute. You want me to answer your questions, but you don't have to answer mine?"

She looked at him pointedly.

"Different girl, yes, but I'm not always that way."

She looked at him pointedly again.

"All right. Enough with the looks," he conceded. "Maybe I have had a bad habit lately of occupying my time with subpar entertainment."

"That's no way to talk about those women."

"No, no," he corrected quickly. "Let me clarify. At

one point, I obviously thought they were great. Otherwise, I would not have been back for seconds."

Her eyes widened. "Rex. You're impossible."

"This isn't coming out right. Don't get me wrong, they're all nice girls, I'm sure, but lately, I don't know. It hasn't been enough. I've needed to change things up a bit. I've been going through the motions for a while and, quite frankly, I'm getting tired of the same old routine."

"Then why don't you stop?"

"Because it is almost too easy. What man in their right mind turns downs sex for no reason?" he asked.

"Maybe a respectable one."

"Maybe," he agreed.

Silence elapsed between them.

"Well, it looks like the coast is clear. No boogey man is going to come peeking out from behind any corners. I even checked underneath the bed."

At the mention of her bed, her cheeks flushed. *Stop being so juvenile*, she chided herself.

He moved toward her. "Why do you get so flushed at the mention of me in your bedroom?"

Kit's hands flew protectively to her chest to stop him. "Stop doing that," she warned.

"Doing what?" Rex asked innocently.

"Sexualizing everything."

"I do not do any such thing."

"We just got finished having a conversation about how you're trying to overcome giving in to easiness of falling into bed with every single eligible woman in town."

"Okay, you got me there, but you should know I have not been with every woman in town."

His eyes peered into hers.

"Smooth, Mr. Jennings, but I intend for it to stay that way."

"Relax, Kit, maybe we could just have a drink, between two adults. Just conversation from someone who challenges me, I promise. Besides, I saw you had some beer in your refrigerator."

She hesitated.

"You won't offer me a beer after I helped you get into your cabin, behaved myself in your classroom, and searched your house for you? I don't deserve a drink in your company? Or is that too much to ask?"

Kit bit her lip, contemplating what the most responsible course of action should be.

"Forget it, I'll just go." He started to make his way toward the door.

Before Kit had time to rethink her actions her arm reached out and snatched his shirt sleeve.

He stopped without turning to look at her.

"You don't have to go. You can stay."

His head swiveled back toward her in disbelief. "I can?"

"For a drink. For one drink," she said sternly.

"Thank you, ma'am, for your hospitality. That's the best offer I have had in a long time," he said sarcastically.

"Take it or leave it," she replied coolly.

Kit turned and made her way to the kitchen.

"I'll take it. All right, all right."

She retrieved two beverages and, after rifling through the drawers, she finally found a bottle opener.

Popping the top, she handed him a beer, and he took a swig, draining the neck.

"You better savor it, Romeo, remember I was firm on one drink. I've got unpacking to do, and I can't be distracted."

Rex smiled, reassured. "So you think I'm a distraction?"

"Don't humor yourself. It wasn't mean as a compliment."

"Still, I'll take it."

☙❧☙

When they popped the top on their third drink, he asked. "Do you want to go out on the dock?"

"Isn't it kind of cold?"

"Do you own a coat? Besides, we have some of the best stars this time of year. It's a real sight to be seen. You should lighten up, teach. If this is going to be your home now, you should learn to enjoy yourself."

Do not fall for his charm. This is what he does with all of the girls.

"So are you coming with me or what?"

Don't do it, Kit, the voice inside of her head screamed.

She started to shake her head no and caught a glimpse of the gift bag that she'd set on the counter. "Okay, let's go," she answered.

"Really?"

"Don't look so surprised. Let's go before I change my mind. I'm just going to grab my coat."

Kit went on a manhunt through boxes labeled winter. As she rifled through them, Rex wandered around the maze of boxes, peering in and moving around items here and there out of curiosity.

"Found it." Kit turned around and stopped short. "Don't look in there," she demanded sharply.

"Whoa, I'm sorry. Whose things are these?"

Kit crossed the room and slammed the top of the box shut. "None of your business," she said, emphasizing each word slowly.

"Okay, but those things obviously belong to a male and using my very astute detective skills, judging by the style of clothing it would not be your father's. Who did you leave behind, Kit?'

"I don't want to talk about it." Kit sucked in her breath, hoping he would leave it alone.

"Fine, we will not talk about it. Let's go see some stars."

She breathed a sigh of relief and followed him out the front door and down the dark path toward the water.

The crisp air was cool enough that they could see their breaths expel from their mouths, like smoke rings, taking on different patterns in the night air.

"It is so dark out here."

"Are you scared? You can lean in close if you want."

"Please, the only thing I have to be scared of is you. It's chillier than I thought out here."

"Do you ever stop complaining?"

"I'm not complaining, just stating facts."

"Whatever you call it, stop talking and look up," he said

Kit reached out and slapped his arm, but did as he told her and stared up at the night sky. The sky was clear and the stars glinted like diamonds creating a million constellations that on a cloudy night would hide from view.

"Wow," she breathed.

"It is a real beauty, huh?'

"Yes, thank you for sharing it with me," she whispered.

He grabbed her hand. "Come on, it is even better on the dock."

They walked cautiously down the steps in the dark. Kit laughed and suddenly missed the bottom stair.

She shrieked in surprise. Rex caught her arm.

"Watch it. You okay?"

She was bent over and her body was shaking.

"What? Did you twist your ankle?"

When she brought her head up, she was laughing.

For a moment he just stared at her, enchanted with the melody of the joyous sound escaping her lips. She was laughing so that tears rolled down her cheeks.

Rex could not help, but laugh along with her, and he reached out and brushed a lone tear off of her cheek tenderly. The move had been impulsive and caused her to stop short. The laughter subsided, and she glanced away uncomfortably.

"Don't stop," he whispered.

"What?" she asked.

"Laughing. It's beautiful."

She was taken off guard by his words and her astonishment showed. "What are you doing?"

"Paying you a compliment. Is that not allowed?"

"Of course, it's allowed." She shifted her weight. "It makes me nervous."

He leaned forward. "Why do I make you nervous?"

"Because you're dangerous," she said quietly.

"Dangerous. I've never gotten that one before. Here I was actually trying to be respectable."

"You respectable?" She meant it sarcastically, but it came out as a whisper.

He raised his hand to cup her chin and stroked her cheek with his thumb. His fingertips were rough against her smooth porcelain skin.

Her breath hitched in her throat, and he reacted without preamble. His mouth claimed hers and took her by surprise. Being caught off guard, she did not have time to stop him.

He meant to be slow and gentle, but once he felt her lips move in return, he could not stop himself. A soft moan escaped her lips, and he deepened the kiss, parting her lips with his tongue. She opened her mouth to allow her entry and some small part of him was surprised that she was willingly kissing him back instead of slapping him.

His hands wrapped around her and, as big as they were, they nearly encircled her small frame. Her arms moved from being stationary at her sides to move up around his neck. Her fingers played with his hair that was slightly too long at the base of his neck, and that drove him mad.

He backed her up against the post along the dock, feeling as much of her body through the heavy coat as he could. When she was leaning against the supportive guard rail, he used his nimble fingers to find the zipper and impatiently worked it down to give him more access to her body.

His hands found their way beneath her shirt, and he felt the soft skin above her jeans. He squeezed her hips as he kissed her hard on the mouth.

She raked her nails through his hair, breathing heavily, and made circular movements with her hips against him. Through the pelvic thrusts and denim material, she could feel the bulge that had been created through their friction. It may have been cold, but neither of them noticed as their mounting passion intensified.

He spun her around to face the water and spooned her from behind, cupping her breasts and nuzzling her earlobe and then her neck.

His hands kneaded her small mounds and the points were perky and alert. She moaned gratefully and arched in unison with the rhythm of his motions.

She was hot, and he did not expect this kind of reaction out of her. He was ready and losing patience quickly. He slipped his hand beneath her waistband and inside of her panties. When he felt her she was soft and inviting. His fingers entered her and she pressed herself against him, letting out a pleasurable gasp.

She felt good and he enjoyed touching her. Her body tightened around his fingers and he felt the shudders from the inside out. Her body quaked, and she gasped with release. The aftershocks flickered throughout her body until they gradually subsided.

Before he could turn her around to continue their foreplay, her body went rigid.

Rex knew before she spoke a switch had been flipped.

"Please stop."

"What?" he asked, perplexed.

"I can't."

"What do you mean you can't? I believe you just did."

"I know. I'm sorry." She fumbled with the button on her jeans. "It was not supposed to happen. I do not know what got into me."

"I know what got into you." He stared at her hard in the eye.

"You know what I mean. I am not usually so—"

"Fun?"

She looked away from him.

"When was the last time a man touched you like that?"

She looked back at him miserably.

"Let me guess. You are going to say that it's none of my business."

"No. It's not. Look, I know it's unfair for me to…" She struggled to find the words. "…and not for you to…"

"Get off? Come on, do not get all shy on me now. You were not the polished ice queen a few minutes ago."

"I said I was sorry. Can we just pretend like this never happened?"

"Easy for you to say. You got yours, and I still have a bulging erection to take care of."

He was angry, confused, and couldn't stop himself, although the look on her face was one of misery and mortification.

"I'm sure you can call one of your many hook ups to take care of that for you. Take them to look at the stars. I'm sure it is all part of your routine."

Her cheeks were pink and her eyes flashed angry, but shone bright under the moonlit sky with unshed tears.

"Are you that horrified that you could derive so much pleasure from a simple Southern backwoods bartender? What has got you, huh? I mean, I did not even have to work that hard to get you going. The ice queen melted fast. It must have been a while because it was awfully—"

"Easy?" she finished for him. "I'm not horrified with you. This is all just part of your regular programming. I'm horrified at myself for my lapse in judgment and not trusting what I already knew."

"Oh yeah, and what's that?"

"That you're not respectable at all."

She turned and hurried up the dark walk way back to her cabin.

ᴄᴏᴄᴏ

He sat in the distance bundled up and blew on his hands to keep them warm.

The little scene he had witnessed was interesting. For a second there, he thought he was about to have a front row seat to an amateur porno. Unfortunately, Kit cut the show short, ranting and raving about something and the guy was mad, for obvious reasons.

With a little recon work, he'd figured out that the man named Rex was her neighbor.

Well, if she thought that moving on was on the agenda, she thought wrong. If he could not move on, then neither could she. Life was not fair and he thought showing that to her a year ago would be enough for him, but it had not been. His pain and resentment still ran deep.

He would be damned if he still had to live in misery, but she could move on to find happiness, or maybe another love. No, life was not fair at all, and he would not stop until they were all as miserable as he was.

He had found contentment when she still lived in Watertown, and he could visibly see her wallow in her self-pity and fear. He had even almost convinced himself that would be enough, but not now.

She wanted a fresh start. He planned to show Ms. Harwick that she could run, but she could not hide. He would remind her that the past would always be with her the same way it haunted him.

He rather liked her scared and vulnerable, and he planned to keep her that way until he put an end to it once and for all. You had to be careful who you associated with, and she had paid the price for being with Officer Slade. Now Rex Jennings would learn the same lesson for being with her.

Kit was damaged goods, and he would not stop until she was destroyed just as much as he was.

He got aroused just thinking about it and crouched down in the shadows of the long willow branches. He even thought about touching himself as he watched her through her window as she innocently change into her bed clothes, but he was not a guy of instant gratification. At least, not anymore. He sat like that until the bedroom lights clicked off, and then he slowly made his way around the bend to his hidden pickup truck. Around these parts, the vehicle was a dime a dozen, and no one would have cause to be suspicious, but even so, he had made sure it did not stick out enough to be noticed.

Before he pulled out onto the highway, he made a pit stop at Mr. Jennings's cabin. He shoved the paper bag into the correct mailbox and closed the metal door. As he pulled away, he smiled to himself. His plan was going along perfectly.

He applauded himself silently for his brilliance, self-control, and meticulous patience.

That's when he saw the blonde leaving Rex's house.

"My, my, my. What do we have here?"

CHAPTER 8

Rex had never met a more frustrating woman in his life, and he had encountered his fair share in his time. What was her problem? She was so hot and cold, back and forth, he thought he might be suffering from whiplash.

He should just cut his losses and go back to his uncomplicated existence, but somehow that seemed unfulfilling and less appealing now. That left him agitated and pissed off. He had been given the green light, then just as he stepped on the gas, another road block had been thrown up, slapping him with no warning at all.

He could have had an outlet with Lisa who had once again shown up unannounced, but instead of being appeased with a backup plan, he was annoyed that she had taken it upon herself to assume he would be ecstatic at the sight of her and be quick to roll over and play stud.

Rex knew that was what was expected of him, and, normally, he was happy to oblige, but somehow it seemed meaningless now. More meaningless than casual sex usually was. It now made him feel shallow and like he had never considered that all of his actions had consequences. He had never considered that the women he slept with might actually have feelings for him or that falling into bed with them after a few too many cocktails might actually be hindering him from reaching his full potential.

He also never pondered the idea as to why, in order to act on these random rendezvous, he had to be in a booze-induced haze, and the less he knew about them, the better.

It made him question what he had been doing the last couple of years. How it must appear to her. He was reduced to a bartender with no goals in life, other than to pick up random chicks any night of the week, drinking in the hopes to have a dreamless sleep and escape the reality of the past and the unknown of the future.

Rex had never cared how he appeared to others. Who cared if they thought he was a good looking guy who lacked ambition but charmed his way through life and with the ladies? There was some truth to it, of course, wasn't there? He had made the reputation for himself, and now he was stuck with it.

So why now did he wish like hell he had not sealed his own fate? Was all this self-loathing a result of being turned down by one complicated woman? Certainly, it could not be. She obviously had enough skeletons in her closet that she refused to talk about. She was a very layered person, and just when he thought he was making progress, the next layer was more confusing than the last.

No, it was not all Kit's rejection that had him second guessing his life choices. He had been spinning his wheels for a while, but he had to admit that her obvious disapproval was enough to spark him into acknowledging his own dissatisfaction with his stagnant lifestyle.

Truth be told, he did not get turned down often, and his own reaction to the concept came as a complete surprise to him. He was pouting like a pubescent teenager, and he knew it, but what was even more frustrating was that he was powerless to stop it.

All he knew was that two women were now mad at him; one of which he tried to sleep with and the other tried to sleep with him. At the end of the day, everyone was frustrated, confused, and no one got laid.

Rex stomped angrily to the kitchen and reached into the refrigerator for a cold beer. He popped the top and, without closing the door, took a long drink from the bottle. Out of the corner of his eye, he saw red and blue flashing lights coming toward his window.

"What the hell?"

He made his way toward his kitchen window and watched the whirl of lights come closer and then turn suddenly around the bend. They were headed toward the houses past him, and he let himself out onto the deck to see where they were going. The car was traveling at higher speeds than these roads really allowed but stopped quickly, arriving at its emergent destination.

"Shit."

He set his beer down and grabbed for his coat before running in the same direction.

Kit.

His mind raced faster than his legs could carry him as he headed toward her cabin.

His chest hurt and his throat burned as he sucked in the cold air. He skidded to a halt when he saw her sitting on the front step, and relief washed over him when he saw her wide-eyed and petite frame sitting on the front stoop. He covered his face with his hands and expelled a long breath, sure that the look on his face was evidence of the mounting fear he felt on the short run to her house.

When she looked up from her position on the steps, she appeared shocked to see him there.

Her surprise was written on her face and the fear was

evident on his. For a moment neither of them spoke.

"Are you okay?" he asked breathlessly.

"What are you doing here?" Her voice cracked.

"Yeah. What are you doing here?" Brady seconded.

It was the first time Rex turned his attention to the officer. "Not that it's any of your business, but I saw the way you tore down the road, like a bat out of hell, I figured something must be terribly wrong." He turned his attention back toward Kit. "When I saw him pull up in front of your house, I thought..." He trailed off. "Well, I do not know what I thought, but after you had me search your place earlier, anyway, are you okay?" he asked again.

"Physically? Yes, I am fine," she said quietly as she rubbed her arms to ward off the chill.

He was reminded that not long before, his hands were touching her skin. He'd felt the chill bumps raise across her body as much from being turned on as from the lowering temperatures.

The way her eyes purposefully avoided his and the way her cheeks flushed told him that she was remembering too.

They had exchanged heated words, but seeing that their recent slip of intimacy had an effect on her provided him with a small amount of satisfaction.

"So if you're okay, then why did you call the police?"

"Rex, I have barely had time to ask any questions myself. Maybe you just want to back away and let me do my job."

Rex clenched his fist and his jaw pulsed. He ignored the officer and went back to questioning Kit. "Does this have to do with the package that was left on the porch? Is that why you had me search through your house?"

"What package? When did you search her house?

Will someone fill me in on what is going on? I cannot very well help if I'm left in the dark."

"You probably would not be much help anyway, Deputy Dooey," Rex said sarcastically.

"That is enough out of you." Brady pointed his flash-light at him for emphasis.

"Or what? Are you going to zap me with your laser beam?"

"I've got a mind to do much worse than that if you do not shut your trap."

"Man, I better behave myself. I'm really worried."

"Rex, do you always have to make yourself out to be an ignoramus? I'm still trying to figure out if the washed up bartender routine is all an act to make people feel sorry for you or is that really your highest potential?"

Rex lunged toward the officer and gripped him up by his shirt collar. Brady did not even have time to reach for his taser. "Now, you listen to me, you son of a bitch. Some of us were not born with a silver spoon in our mouths, and my life is none of your concern."

"Are we really going down this road again? If you do not let go of me, I have got a mind to just drop your ass right here."

"I would like to see you try."

"Guys, guys. Stop. Please stop."

The men turned their attention back toward Kit. The reason they were both here in the first place.

Rex reluctantly released his grip on Brady's shirt collar, and Brady angrily smoothed it and shoulder checked him as he tried to regain his air of professional-ism.

"I'm sorry you had to witness that immature display of machoism. How can I help you? The dispatcher said it was somewhat of an emergency."

Kit felt mildly embarrassed but then reminded herself that these two men had just acted out a testosterone-driven childhood feud right before her eyes for reasons that obviously began long ago and were not apparent to her, although neither of them had seemed to grow up much since.

"That is what I told the dispatcher, yes, but now I think I might have over exaggerated a bit. I was already a bit frazzled." She nervously glanced toward Rex, and it did not go unnoticed by the policeman.

"Go on, Rex, get out of here." Brady motioned for him to go. "Give the lady some privacy."

Rex hesitated briefly and, sensing he had no other choice but to comply, turned to walk away. "You have got to be kidding me. This is ridiculous."

When he was out of earshot Brady motioned for her to continue. "Sorry about that, ma'am. Most neighbors are…well, somewhat neighborly. Please continue."

Kit cleared her throat. "Rex has been fine, really. It is the messages that I have been getting that have me concerned."

"What kind of messages?"

Kit reached into the gift bag that was next to her, and handed him the messages.

Brady's eyes skimmed through the article in the dim glow of the porch light. He looked at her in confusion. "Why are you receiving newspaper articles from Watertown, Illinois, that date back from a year ago, describing an investigation of the death of a police officer?"

Kit squeezed her eyes shut and cleared her throat. "Watertown is where I came from. The officer was ambushed, murdered in cold blood. They never found the person responsible."

"I'm sorry. Did you know him?"

"Officer Anderson Slade was my fiancé."

For a moment neither of them spoke. Sensing he

should stay silent, Brady waited for her to continue.

"He was on the night shift and had met with some of his coworkers at the station. Someone had staked them out with a high-powered scope rifle. They literally buzzed him in and, when the doors opened, he took his shot. Andy never saw it coming."

"I'm so sorry, Kit. I had no idea."

"That is because I asked Mellie not say anything. I wanted a chance to start over. This past year has been...well, challenging to say the least. When Mellie suggested I move down here, I decided a change of pace was exactly what I needed." Kit pondered the very words that had just escaped her lips. "That's not entirely true. At first, I did not really want to leave the place I called home. I felt it somehow kept me connected to Andy, but, as I stated, Andy's killer was never caught and living in a constant state of paranoia is no way to live, let me tell you."

"I cannot imagine. That must have been terrible for you."

"So here I am, in a different state, where I do not really know anyone besides Mellie, and no one knows me, ready for a fresh start, praying for one actually. But it seems you cannot really escape the past."

"No, unfortunately, you can't," Brady agreed. "What is going on now? Is someone threatening you?"

"I wouldn't say threatening. That may be too broad of a term. But the other morning I was out for a run, and when I came back this package was sitting on my stoop. I am fairly positive it was not there when I left. It was not postmarked so it was a personal delivery and not made by a mail service. It was an article rehashing all of the gory details of the case. It left me unsettled, but overall I figured someone who knew my past wanted to keep me abreast of any new developments, but then the other night my keys went missing, granted I was at Middy's so I could have simply overindulged and misplaced them, but something did not seem right.

"Rex helped pick the lock so that I could get in, but today another package was left here and, as you already saw, it was an article saved from a year ago. I'm not sure what kind of message they're trying to send me or who's trying to send it. But tonight, I stepped out for a second." She hesitated. "We took a walk around the dock. When I returned, my door was standing open. It was pretty windy so maybe it was not shut completely. But a little while ago, I was standing in the kitchen and heard a noise. It sounded like it was coming from overhead. I am not going to lie, I panicked and did not wait to see where it was coming from, nor did I search to find out. I got out of there as fast as my legs could carry me."

"Rightfully so. You did the right thing by calling us. I would be glad to check it out for you."

"I admit it seems more likely that it was just a bad case of the nerves."

"Even so, Kit, I'll check it out and let's hope that's all it was. The door being left open could easily be explained by the wind. It's awfully windy, and these latches are old. As far as the messages, I'll make a copy of them and start a file. If you ever have to call again, we'll already know the background to save you from having to rehash it all again. We can add some extra patrols around your neck of the woods, and you should feel comfortable calling us anytime. That's what we're here for."

"Thank you, Officer Renshaw. I appreciate that very much."

"Call me Brady please. And if you are ever in a crisis, you should run to Rex Jennings's house until we can get here."

"Rex?" she asked, perplexed. "That's odd, considering you two appear to hate each other."

"Hate is a strong word. However, strongly dislike is pretty accurate. But we would not be brothers without a scuffle or two."

"Brothers?" She could not contain her surprise.

"Half-brothers," Brady clarified.

"Huh, I didn't see that one coming."

CHAPTER 9

Kit watched Brady do a three point turnabout and gave a little friendly wave as he drove away. She blew out a deep breath and paused to stare at the night sky. This had to be one of the longest days, and she had many of them after Andy was gone.

Silence enveloped the darkness around her, except the occasional sound of an animal in the woods or the breeze rippling off of the pond. It was eerie, but no more eerie than going back inside of her house, even after Brady searched it thoroughly, room by room.

She looked across the pond in the direction of Rex's cabin. It was dark, and she wondered what he thought about her after tonight, but wondering was pointless, and she reluctantly turned on her heel to make her way back inside.

"Why didn't you tell me?"

Startled, she nearly jumped out of her own skin, as a figure merged from the shadows. "Rex." She breathed a sigh of relief. "Have you been there the whole time?"

He walked out of the hedges, jamming his hands in his pockets as he came. "Why didn't you tell me?" he asked again.

Her face dropped, as she struggled to find the words, finally raising her hands in unexplained exasperation. She tried to speak, but no sound came out as emotions threatened to overwhelm her. He was by her side in two strides. "What was I supposed to say?" she whispered. "We barely know each other."

"Right, but I would not have been such an ass. This explains some things."

"Well, you have proven you can definitely be an ass, but really what would you have done differently?"

He smirked. "I deserve that, but I would have been more…" He searched for the right thing to say.

"Respectable?" she finished for him.

"Maybe, or at least I would try to be."

"Something tells me that's not your forte."

"In any event, I'm sorry for some of the things that I said. You can blame my ego."

Kit nodded, not wanting to rehash the argument after their intimate encounter.

"Let me ask you, why didn't you tell me that Officer Renshaw was your brother?"

"Half-brother, and, as you have already stated, we barely know each other, and it did not seem relevant."

"Fair enough. You guys argue like you're still in your pubescent years."

"Probably worse, and I don't see it getting any better any time soon."

"Which parent do you share, and did you fight like this as children?"

"We share a father, if that is what you would call him, and what is this, twenty questions?"

"Sorry, I'm just curious."

"Look, he and I try to stay out of each other's way, but enough talking about old history that is too late to change. Are you okay?"

"Yes." She sighed and her breath was visible accumulation of carbon monoxide. "At least I think so. My house has been searched twice in one night. It better be safe, right?"

She gave a nervous laugh.

"Do you think that someone tried to get into your house tonight, while we were at the dock?"

"I don't know what to think. Maybe I'm just paranoid, but I do know that someone is trying to relay a message to me by leaving me articles from the case, and whether it's meant to or not, it's freaking me out."

He squeezed her arms. "That's understandable, but who would do something like that?"

She shook her head sadly. "I don't know and, for whatever reason, it appears that they do not want me to know either." She shivered.

"It's cold, you better go back inside. You're safe now. I'll wait until you lock the doors. If you need anything, you know how to reach me."

She started up the porch steps and hearing them creek beneath her was enough to unsettle her further. She spun around impulsively. "Rex?"

"Yeah?"

"Do you mind staying a while? Until I fall asleep? I know it is silly, but—"

"I can do that," he said genuinely.

He started up the stairs and something in her belly churned. Kit already second guessed her decision.

"Whoa, just platonic okay? We already saw what happened when we…" She blushed. "You know."

Rex smiled. "I can keep my hands to myself. The real question is can you?"

She gave him a look.

"Okay, platonic. I got the message loud and clear. No need to get all hot and bothered."

"I am not blushing," she exclaimed.

"Oh, I guess it must be the heat." Rex fanned himself sarcastically.

"I'm glad you're so tickled by all of this."

Rex stopped laughing. "I'm not tickled by the circumstances, Kit. I'm sorry for your loss, and I'm willing to help."

"Thank you. I appreciate it more than you know." Her voice was husky, and Rex locked the door behind them.

༄༅༄

From somewhere in the distance another pair of eyes was watching.

"Tsk, tsk. Barely in town a week and inviting a man to stay. This is not what I had in mind." He turned his attention to the wide-eyed blonde sitting beside him. "It kind of puts a damper on your plans with Mr. Jennings, too, doesn't it?"

Lisa gritted her teeth and nodded in agreement.

༄༅༄

"Are you okay?"

"Yes, I appreciate you staying with me."

Rex grinned. "It is not a hardship, trust me."

Kit ducked her head sheepishly. "Well, nevertheless, I don't think I could handle being alone tonight."

"You don't have to be," he said huskily.

Kit saw the suggestive look in his eyes. "Platonic, remember? We can be friends."

"Right, friends. I can't say I've been in the practice

of being 'just friends' with very many females."

Kit laughed. "Maybe it's time you start."

"Maybe. Probably."

"I'm not ruining any big plans with any of those females, am I?"

Rex thought about how Lisa had been waiting for him at his cabin. "No, you're not ruining anything."

"Good. I've got some blankets set out on the couch. Feel free to watch the television or raid my fridge. Although, I do not have much to offer, only what Mellie stocked before I got here. I think there's some beer left."

"Great, thanks. Are you and Mellie close?"

"Proximity while growing up made it somewhat difficult, but not for lack of her trying. She has always been loving and consistent. It was my parents who were somewhat..." She paused. "Well, that's another story, and it has been a long day. I don't think I can rehash anymore of my emotional turmoil. I have more than met my quota for the day."

"Fair enough."

She paused.

"Look, teach, don't feel like you have to stay up to entertain me."

"Okay, I am exhausted."

Rex stood up and leaned in for an awkward hug.

"Thank you again."

He got a whiff of her hair and breathed in the sweet smell. He lingered a moment too long. "No problem," he whispered.

She pulled back reflexively.

"Don't worry, platonic, I got it," Rex repeated.

"Good night," she said hurriedly and rushed out of the room.

What made her think that Rex Jennings could ever be capable of a platonic relationship?

Kit slid under the covers and laid her head against her pillow. Her brain was fried. She should have been able to close her eyes and drift into a dreamless slumber, but her mind was racing, going a hundred miles per hour, and she was powerless to control the direction of her thoughts.

She was being controlled by fear, fear of the unknown, fear of Andy's killer, fear of the person seeking her out with messages and what their motive could possibly be. Fear of fitting in to a new place where she would be forced to let go of the past. On top of the all-consuming fear, she was confused. Confused by this fresh start she was supposed to be making, confused by the neighbor that was sleeping in the other room on her couch. He was virtually a stranger and yet they had shared a moment so intimate and personal, she was confused with herself about how she let that happen.

She missed Andy so much it hurt and, although she had learned how to survive in a world without him, she feared she would never truly live. Would she have hopes and dreams, happiness and success, or would she remain a shell of a person, going through the motions, putting on a brave, but emotionless face for the outside world?

Rex had called her cold, and it had hurt her feelings, but mainly because, as rude as he was, he was right.

She hadn't always been that way. She had been warm, caring, and funny. She loved to laugh until her cheeks hurt, to feel passionate about something, to feel love, and to make love.

Then the rug was ripped out from underneath her. Now she was passionate about one thing—finding Andy's killer and seeing that justice was served. It seemed that someone else was determined to make sure she did not forget it either.

She could not figure out if this person was friend or

foe. Did this person mean to aide or destruct? She felt as if she was already on a clear path to self-destruction all on her own. When Andy first passed, she dreamed of closing her eyes and just not waking up. If she willed it hard enough, maybe her soul would escape her body and relieve her of the pain, allowing her to be with Andy again.

Try as she might, she continued to wake up day after day, forced to face another day until, eventually, she realized her story was not finished yet. She owed it to Andy and herself to see what was left for her in this world. Andy would have wanted her to be happy.

There was a purpose for her here on Earth, and she would be doing her creator, herself, and Andy an injustice if she did not try to find out what the purpose was. She moved here, in part, to escape and, in part, to find a new identity. She realized she had failed in escaping, and she was not sure who she wanted to be yet, but she had felt alive, felt the butterflies, nervous anxiety.

It was a relief to be able to feel something—anything—however, the person who had forced her to confront these awakening emotions that were stirring from a long hibernation was just on the other side of the wall. He had reminded her that she was human, a female with desires, vulnerabilities, but he also infuriated her and challenged her, and insulted her even while lending a hand. She was not sure if she was prepared for the complications of rejoining the real world.

She might not like it, but worse, she might realize she did not like herself. Damn him for making her question herself.

She flung back the covers and started into the other room.

CHAPTER 10

Y
ou said I was cold."

He looked up at her in surprise. "Yes."

"That I was an ice queen."

"Yes," he answered quietly.

"You saw me as a snotty, whiney, girl who selfishly let you please her without returning the favor."

"Kit, don't do that."

"Don't do what? Bring up your opinion of me? I was easy and a tease, right?"

"Kit, that was before—"

"Before, what? You found out my fiancé was murdered? Now you feel sorry for me."

"Kit, it was before I knew what you had been through."

"And now you feel sorry for me, right?"

"No, yes. I mean I'm sorry for what you have been through. I would not be human if I wasn't, but I should not have said what I said, regardless of your past history. You said stop. You weren't interested. It's fine. I understand. I told you that it was my ego talking. I admit I was a little defensive."

Kit took a deep, but shaky, breath. "I was not always

this way. You know, I don't know why I even care what you think, but I wanted you to know that. I aspired to be things, do things. People described me as friendly and warm. I was dependable. I wanted to travel and be a wife and a mother. I was a lot of things but I was not cold. I was not a tease or an ice queen." Her voice cracked with unbridled emotion. "I was happy."

The tears that had pooled in her eyes spilled over and rolled down her cheeks. Rex stood suddenly and grabbed her in a tight hug.

"Don't." She resisted. "Don't be nice to me."

"Would it be so bad if I was nice to you? Please let me help you," Rex said soothingly.

"Yes, it would be bad."

"Why?" He tilted her face so that she could not avoid his questioning gaze.

Her expression was pained. "Because I do not need your pity. Or anyone else's, for that matter."

Rex continued to wrap his arms around her. "It is going to be okay. You will be happy again one day. Truly happy. You have suffered a scare and you are in a new place. Cut yourself a break. That would be pretty overwhelming for anybody. We'll get it figured out, and I'm sure there's a logical explanation for the messages. The police will give you extra patrols and you're safe."

She sniffed. "I thought you did not think very highly of the police."

"Just because I do not care for one of them on a personal level does not mean I do not trust them on a professional one. Brady may be a lot of things, but he's a thorough investigator. As much as it pains me to pay him any kind of compliment, he is good at his job."

"Well, what if I did not tell him everything?"

"What do you mean?"

She reached into the bag that she had brought out

from the bedroom and hesitated only briefly before drawing out the cutouts.

"What are these?" he asked, confused.

"I think they're pieces to a picture. When I received the first message, I did not think much about it, but when I saw the same similar cutout image in the second message, I knew it could not be a coincidence. You see the edges of the images are clipped like a makeshift jigsaw puzzles, and these two pieces fit together to make a part of a corner, or a border."

Rex leaned down and studied the glossy paper. "It looks like you're right, but what is it an image of?"

"I'm not sure, but it obviously has something to do with the newspaper articles or Andy's death."

Rex contemplated what she was saying.

"What are you thinking?" she asked him. "I knew it. You think I'm over reacting, that I'm crazy." She started to pace. "Hell, I probably am crazy."

He grabbed her arm. "Hey, I don't think that you're crazy. Not at all. I agree with you that the puzzle picture is some kind of hidden message. I'm just not sure what they're trying to say. Why didn't you give this to the police?"

"I honestly don't know? They said they were going to make copies of the articles so that they could put it in their files. I wanted to keep to keep any clues I could to figure this out."

Rex nodded his understanding, although he didn't really understand at all. "I'll help in any way that I can, but I'm no Brady Renshaw. I'm just a small town bartender, but I'll do my best."

"Now that you mention it. Why did you leave the fire department in New York? That is a very sought-over position. Whatever made you leave such a promising career?"

"It's a long story."

"That you would rather not tell me about?"

"No, I would just rather not talk about it at all."

"Okay, fine. I'm sorry I pried. I guess I just thought we were sharing life stories. You now know my vulnerabilities and that's fine. You do not have to share. I'm going back to bed. I'll see you in the morning."

"Kit, don't be like that."

"Be like what?" She stopped at the doorway. "I'm not being like anything, absolutely nothing at all. Like I said, feel free to make yourself comfortable."

She closed her bedroom door with a defiant click.

∽∾∽

"How is the writing going?"

"I think I have some writer's block going on. My brain focuses on just about everything other than the story."

"Come on, Kitty Kat. You know that you can't force these things. It'll come to you and, when it does, the words will flow from the pen so fast your hands won't be able to keep up."

She looked up him, smiling. "Who's the writer?"

"What do you say you take a break, and I'll give you something to write about?"

He bent down and nuzzled her neck.

"Andy," she squealed. "I really don't have time. My agent will kill me if I don't deliver something soon."

"Good for you, this won't take long, and good for me, it's a good excuse for it not lasting too long."

Kit laughed and allowed herself to be lead away from the computer.

Andy kissed her playfully, stopping to nibble her ear.

"I've missed you," he said tenderly. "This working opposite shifts has been driving me crazy."

"I agree. It's been too long."

He pulled his shirt over his head and reclaimed her mouth, lowering her onto the desk.

"Two thirty-seven can you call dispatch?" the radio screeched.

"Ten-four."

Andy pulled his work phone from his pants.

"I thought you did not have to go in until later tonight."

"I didn't, but we're down two guys tonight, so we're shorthanded." Andy smiled grimly. "Hey, what's up? It's Slade."

"Hey, we have a possible domestic disturbance. Neighbors reported hearing loud shouting. Suspect has history of aggressive behavior, and we've been warned he's most likely off of his meds. Apparently, suspect has a scanner and has been known to obsessively tune in. Officers need back up, but you need to communicate privately, so he doesn't have advanced notice that you're coming. How soon can you be out?"

Andy looked at his watch and back at Kit. "I'll be out in two. Tell the guys I'm on my way."

"Will do. Also note that subject is most likely armed and exhibits erratic behavior."

"Ten-four. I'll be there shortly."

He threw his undershirt back on and grabbed his gun belt as he zipped up his tactical boots.

Kit followed him, grabbing his vest and squad car keys as he went.

"Thank you, babe. We'll pick up where we left off later." He kissed her quickly on the mouth.

"Just please be careful."

"Always am, but duty calls."

He pulled down their driveway, running hot with sirens and lights, as she waved from the porch, watching him speed away.

☙☙☙

"I'm not really sure that this is something I want to be a part of," Lisa said nervously.

"What are you talking about? Apart of what? What are we doing wrong?"

She licked her lips. "Whatever this is, spying on them, peeping in their windows without their knowledge. It seems wrong."

He seemed to take in what she said. "Is it wrong to want to know what is going on behind out backs? He practically dismissed your standing date for that cold-hearted floozy underneath your nose without so much as an explanation."

She fidgeted uncomfortably. "That may be exaggerating a bit. Rex did not really know that I was going to pop in. We would sometimes get together after a late night."

"And it's okay with you that he uses you like that? Blatantly uses you to feed his sexual appetite and spits you out when he's done?"

She blushed, embarrassment filling her. "I wouldn't say that."

"Oh, what would you say it is then?'

"I mean, I guess we kind of use each other. It's kind of an understanding."

"So it's an understanding that he sees other women, but that you remain exclusive to him? It seems one of you is more invested than the other and that hardly seems fair, if you ask me, but suit yourself."

Lisa clamped her mouth shut and studied Rex through the window. Even looking through binoculars, it was evident that he was engaged in an intense conversation.

A wave of jealousy crashed over her, making her blood boil.

"It's okay to be angry. Anyone in your position certainly would be."

"Someone in my position?"

"Yes, a beautiful woman who is being taken advantage of. Rex is not a stupid man, although it suits him well to have people think his brain is as slow as his Southern drawl. He's a man who wants his cake and to eat it too. He'll keep you hanging on by a thread, throw you a bone every once in a while, just enough to keep you coming back. Is that how you want to be treated, as a dog?"

"Listen, I ain't nobody's dog, and I'll be damned if I play second fiddle to another woman. You're right, I don't deserve to be treated as a doormat."

He smiled. "That's the spirit."

Lisa glanced over at him. "What is your interest in all of this?"

"Never mind, we've got plenty of time to talk about that, but the big question is what are we going to do about this?"

CHAPTER 11

Sobs wracked Kit's body as reality hit, and she emerged from the dream slowly, but harshly. The memories came back to her without warning and, although she would invite Andy back with open arms, she couldn't stand the hollowness that was left when she was brought back to reality, to a world where Andy could no longer touch or hold her. She could not hear his voice. It was too much to bear. She wrapped her arms around her knees and buried her face into her pillow, in an attempt to quiet the sobs as she let her grief overtake her.

When the shaking subsided, she rubbed her grainy eyes and lowered her feet to the floor. Her body physically hurt just holding its own weight. She gripped the wall to aid her as she hiccupped and slowly opened the door, creaking as it went.

When she looked up, Rex was staring back at her, standing silent and shirtless, holding a steaming mug. When their eyes met, she stared at him in question suddenly becoming aware of how she must look.

He was the first to break the silence. "I hope you don't mind. I searched your cabinets and found some tea. It always helps me when I have trouble sleeping."

"Oh, thank you." She fidgeted awkwardly, emotion still threatening to overwhelm her. "Mellie must have stocked them with some southern comforts." She hiccupped again, her voice shook as more tears filled her eyes and she ducked her head so that he wouldn't see.

"Don't do that."

"Do what?"

"Be embarrassed. There's no reason to be." He tilted her chin toward him and she looked him in the eye hesitantly. "Take this, it will make you feel better."

"You Southerners and your tea." She attempted a smile but fell somewhat short.

Kit accepted the warm mug and started toward the kitchen. Rex headed back toward his bed on the sofa.

"You can join me, if you want to that is."

Rex looked at her surprised. "Sure."

She flipped on the lights as he grabbed another cold one from the fridge. She stared into her mug, waiting for it to cool, allowing the steam to rise and produce condensation across her cheeks. "I thought you said tea helps you relax and go to sleep?" she commented, eyeing his beer.

He smirked. "These days I prefer something a little stronger."

"Why is that?" she asked.

"No, no Ms. Harwick. You do not get to do that."

"Do what?" she asked innocently.

"Turn this around on me. We are here to talk about you."

"Why is that? That you get to ask all the questions. We have established that I'm screwed up, but what's your story?"

Rex leaned back in his chair, lifting up the two front legs, balancing on the back ones, and for a brief moment, she imagined the joy she would get from pushing him over and seeing the changes in his cavalier look that was planted across his face.

He sighed. "You aren't screwed up, Kit. You have obviously been through hell, and it's apparent you have not made it through to the other side yet, but you will."

She snorted. "Oh, yeah, how can you be so sure?"

"Because a woman like you deserves better. You deserve to be happy, and one day you will be again."

"You don't know me or anything about my happiness."

"I know enough," he said quietly. "You may be down for now, and rightfully so, but not forever. You're strong. You'll pull yourself out of this darkness."

"How do you know that I'm strong?" she asked stubbornly.

"You really are a challenge, aren't you?"

She raised her chin defiantly, causing him to smile.

"Well, let's see. I know you're strong because you've been through heartache. Strong people don't become that way without experiencing some trials and tribulations. You have to go through the furnace to be molded into something beautiful."

Kit looked away from his knowing eyes.

"I also know that you were strong enough to move away from everything that you know and loved and came to a new town that's completely foreign to make a new life for yourself. That takes guts."

"How do you know I wasn't just running away?"

"I don't, maybe you were, but knowing when to move on and start fresh can be a sign of strength."

"Is that what you did by leaving New York and the career you waited so patiently for? Were you starting over?"

A darkness passed over his face. "Me? No, I was running back to the place I swore I would never return to.

I was proving all the critics right. The firefighter could not cut it in the big league so I came back to my small town to run the local watering hole."

"I do not believe that," she said softly.

"Well, believe what you want, doll face, but don't compare yourself to me. I know what you saw when you met me, and all of it was right," he said bitterly.

She bit her lower lip, having no idea that the simple act was sexy as well and he had to control himself from the unintended invitation. "I don't believe that for a second, Rex. You want to know what I think?"

"Not really, but I bet you plan to tell me."

She ignored his sarcasm. "I think that there's more to you than meets the eye. I think you would love nothing more than for me or anyone else to believe that tough-as-nails rough-exterior persona that you put on."

"Oh, what persona is that?" He asked raising his eyebrows.

"The 'I just want to drink all day and roll around in the hay at night, maybe answer a few fire calls every once in a while to get some thrills' persona. I think you know that there's more to life than catching a buzz, sweet talking women, and nursing a hangover by drinking the hair of the dog. For the life of me, I can't figure out why you don't want more for yourself than that."

"What makes you think I even want that? Are you really so sure that I'm any deeper than that? Maybe you should take me at surface level, what you see is what you get."

"See, that's the problem. I see more than that, or at least I like to think so."

"Wishful thinking on your part, teach. You wouldn't be the first one to be mistaken, and you surely won't be the last."

"Maybe so, but I don't know any man who's so worried about getting laid that he sleeps on his neighbor's couch so that she won't be scared or gets up to make her tea because she's an emotional wreck and had a bad dream."

"How do you know it isn't all part of the ground work, and I am not just trying to get in your pants?"

Kit clamped her mouth shut. "Maybe because I have witnessed firsthand you have no shortage of bedmates, all of which would be much less work and are certain to stroke your ego just the way you like. Let's face it, I've got baggage and have been nothing short of a thorn in your side, yet here you are."

Her eyes gleamed across the kitchen table.

"Maybe I was bored. Maybe it was getting too easy, and I need the challenge."

Both of them fell silent.

"Is that the truth?"

"I guess you'll never know."

Kit looked away.

"Look, I didn't want to argue. As must as you exasperate the hell out of me, I appreciate you being here. I don't want to drag you into my mess so I guess I'll go back to bed."

She stood abruptly and got to the doorway.

"Wait."

She paused.

"There are things. Things you don't know. They've made me an angry man. Things that have nothing to do with you, and yet the more questions you ask, the more I find myself taking them out on you. I am sorry."

She turned back around. "I'm listening."

He rubbed his hands over his face.

"Look, I've never been very good at talking about myself. File it under a list of my never-ending flaws. Can we save it for another day?"

She gnawed at some imaginary skin on her left thumb and pretended to study her nails. "All right. Fine."

"Truce, then." He finished his beer and stared at the empty bottle. "So what was your dream about?"

"What?" she asked, surprised.

"You woke up upset and I overheard you crying. I assumed you had a bad dream."

"I guess you could say that."

"Do they happen often?'

She looked at him. "I guess you could say that," she repeated.

"So what are they about?"

She chose her words carefully. "I wouldn't say that they are all necessarily bad or even scary, but they are usually similar in context."

"Being?" he prodded.

She sighed. "Some of the last days with Andy. Memories. They always start off with him and me, just ordinary life, us talking, spending time together, real conversations that we had."

"And, how do they end?'

"Him being called away to work, always on some emergency that could not wait. The force was shorthanded, so the last year of his life that would happen often. They needed back up, and he was one of the first people they would call. We lived thirty minutes away from city life, but it was more rural, living in the suburbs. Don't get me wrong, definitely larger than this, but the calls usually involved some bar fight, domestic disturbance, or jealous ex in turmoil during a custody battle. Occasionally, it could be some scary stuff, but ultimately we thought we were safe, just far enough away from any real danger. Apparently, not far enough."

"So they really have no leads to anyone who could be responsible for shooting him?"

"No." She shook her head sadly. "I mean, they interviewed people, but none that did not have a solid alibi. As the hours, days, and weeks ticked by, the likelihood became less and less. My biggest fear is that Officer Anderson Slade will land in a cold case file with dust on the jacket and that he will never get justice."

"Maybe with the year anniversary coming up, it'll be reinvestigated, something will be remembered and come to light."

"Maybe," she said, dubious. "I know his fellow officers worked around the clock and want nothing more than the capture his killer. They were family—brothers in blue. They would not let someone walk that killed their own, but unfortunately the facts and evidence just weren't there."

"Kit, do you think the person responsible for killing Andy is the one sending you the messages?"

She paused. "I do, Rex. I really do."

"Well, that means he is slipping up, and the sloppier he gets, the more his trail will be easier to follow. We will get him."

"I hope so," she whispered.

"And that also means you and I are going to be seeing more of each other."

She raised her eyebrows.

"If he is contacting you, I am going to be here," Rex assured her.

Kit nodded solemnly.

"As much as it may be a discomfort to you, you need to think back to the last times spent with Andy and to see if anything stands out in your mind."

"I know and I have, and I will, but like you said, 'There are things.' Things that you don't know and let's save them for another day."

CHAPTER 12

You've been here a week and already got Rex Jennings staying over? And here I thought my granddaughter was a good girl. I know it has been a while, but I guess I was wrong. Kit? You hearing me?"

"Hmm. I'm sorry I must have zoned out. What did you say?"

"You must be tired from the late hours you've been keeping with that neighbor of yours."

Kit's face flushed hot, mortified. "It's not what you think, I swear."

"No need to get all squirrely and embarrassed. You're a grown woman. You do not need my permission to have a boy over. There is no need to be ashamed."

"It's really not like that, Mellie, and I'm not squirrely over Rex Jennings."

"Why not? He's a handsome man. He makes most of the women in this town get all hot and bothered. It would not be a surprise, other than you have already expressed your dislike for the man and his rather unorthodox ways."

"That is just it, Mellie, he may be good looking, but

he knows it. Getting women has obviously never been a problem for him, but he's focused on quantity over quality. That isn't something that I tend to respect. I just needed some help around the house, and he loaned a hand. While I appreciate the help, I don't think I could be interested in a man who I did not respect. So that's all it was. A neighbor helping out the newbie in town."

Mellie clicked her tongue on the roof of her mouth and pondered Kit's words. "Respect, huh? Would you respect a man who left his life and job to come back to a small town that he couldn't wait to get out of in the first place to take care of his momma, until her dying day?"

Kit was stunned into silence.

"I guess he didn't mention that?"

"No, I just assumed...well, I don't know. I thought that..."

"That maybe being a firefighter in New York City was too much responsibility for the Southern wild child, and that he actually preferred topping off drinks because it helped him pick up women."

Kit ducked her head shamefully.

"Don't be so hard on yourself, sweet girl. That's what that stubborn ass wants people to think, but underneath it all, he's really just soft as pudding, a hurt little boy who feels like he has no real ties to anyone."

"How did she pass?"

"It was the cancer that took her. She fought it once, when he was just a boy, and he stepped up and became a man before our very eyes. By the time they found it the second time, it had already spread everywhere. It had come back with a vengeance. Julie knew how much Rex had wanted to get out of Middle Bay and how hard he had worked to be put on the NYFD list. The last thing she wanted to do was jeopardize his future when she already felt guilty enough for his past, but considering she knew that, if treatment did not work, she would not have much time, it forced her hand.

"Rex came to be by her side immediately and encouraged her to fight. And fight that woman did, but once it got to her brain, she said enough was enough. That boy never left her side, and word has it he spent every penny making sure she had the best care possible. He devoted so much of his time to her that when the Lord called her home, he was lost and did not know what to do with himself. That was two years ago, and he's still coping and trying to find himself."

"I had no idea," Kit whispered sadly.

"No, I guess you wouldn't. He does not like anyone to feel sorry for him. He's private in that way."

"And he has no other family? What about Brady? It seems their relationship is strained at best, but could he not really benefit from having a brother to lean on?"

"That's an entirely different story and one that neither boy really speaks about anymore. Brady's a decent man, and you won't hear me say a bad word about him, but his father, on the other hand, is the complete opposite. He had a whirlwind romance with Julie, but it seemed legit, like they truly cared about each other. It was not long before she got pregnant with Rex, and they made plans for a quickie wedding.

"One week before the nuptials were to take place, Jack, Rex's father, abruptly broke off the engagement, announcing that he was back together with his ex and she too was pregnant. The women were due within six weeks of each other, both delivering bouncing baby boys, the difference being one was raised in a home with a doting father who showered him with praise and fulfilled all of his needs and most of his wants.

"The other son was not even graced with his father's presence at the hospital and obtained his mother's maiden name on his birth certificate. They never received a penny of child support and Jack never fought for joint custody. It was as if he just washed his hands of the first family he created, leaving Julie as a young single mother to struggle and figure it out on her own.

"Not to mention, when Julie got sick, he did not so much as reach out to his son or offer to help in anyway. Rex is bitter and rightfully so, but he won't so much as mumble Jack's name to give him any kind of acknowledgement in his life, even if it is only to say something negative, but Brady, on the other hand...well, there has always been an unspoken competitiveness, and probably mostly on Rex's part. Despite Brady's DNA and being brought up by two very selfish people, he turned out all right, but I don't believe that Rex has any desire to have a relationship with him. It's a damn shame that Jack put that on his boys. They can't help who their daddy is."

Kit's head was full from all of the information she had to digest. "This explains a lot actually. Thank you, Mellie."

"Well, I'm glad, but don't go telling Rex I told you all that. I don't think he would appreciate me spouting his business, and you know I don't like to gossip."

At that Kit smiled because there was nothing Mellie liked more than sharking a juicy story. "I won't, Mellie. You have a reputation to uphold." She sighed. *And so does Rex, it seems.*

എോെ

Kit looked over her list a second time after she pulled into the hardware store. She took a deep breath and walked through the automated doors. New beginnings, right? That was what this trip represented.

Andy always took care of things like this, but she could handle picking out some paint and new knobs right? If she was going to stay in the cabin and feel comfortable, it was time she made the house a home.

She wasn't going to let her unknown messenger take that away from her. So she bravely put on a front that said she knew exactly what she was doing. Walking with purpose, she planted herself in front of a million plant samples, quickly lost herself in the shades of similar colors, and debated on an accent wall.

As she was wondering if the colors were true to the samples, she fretted over a finish of eggshell or matte and was oblivious that she was no longer alone in the aisle.

"Hello, Ms. Harwick. Picking up some paint today?"

She nearly jumped out of her skin and gasped in surprise. "Brady. I mean, Officer Renshaw, you startled me." She held her hand to her chest. "I guess I was lost in my indecisiveness. How are you?"

"I am sorry, ma'am. I did not mean to frighten you, and Brady suits me just fine."

"No, it's okay. I was in my own little world. Too many choices can be a little overwhelming." She tried to laugh off her awkward response.

He smiled a genuine smile. "Trying to spruce up your place, I reckon."

"Yes, something like that. Nothing a little tic can't fix."

"The other night was the first time I had been in Mellie's cottages in quite some time. They surely are nice, but a little woman's touch could go a long way."

Kit blushed easily and mentally chided herself to not read into his comments or imagine insinuations that surely were not there.

Brady noticed immediately he had made her uncomfortable. "In any event, I'm sure you will be happy when everything is put in its place and decorated the way you like."

"Yes, the chore seems never ending, but in time, I'm sure it will all come together."

They fell into a silence, and she pretended to gaze down at the array of colors in her hand, but she was no longer seeing them at all.

Brady cleared his throat. "So how have you been, Kit?"

Her head popped back up to meet his eyes. "Fine," she lied.

"No more messages being dropped off on your stoop?"

"Not since the other night and thank you, by the way, for coming out and handling that. I'm sure I was just being silly. I thought that someone…well, I was just freaked out. Thank you for putting my mind at ease."

"Anytime, Kit. That's my job. Never hesitate to call. I'll be glad to come out any time, day or night. You don't strike me as a silly woman, and I know you have been through a lot. Besides, it's not really a hardship helping out a pretty woman. I'm glad to do it."

Kit flushed pink again and avoided his eyes.

"I'd be happy to help in other ways as well. Painting, I mean," he quickly clarified.

"Oh, I couldn't ask you to do that," she rushed.

"It's really no trouble at all, or maybe dinner even, if you're up to it."

She opened her mouth, but no words came out.

"Just think about it. You don't have to answer me right away. Besides work, my schedule is fairly open, and I would love to take you out. Just say you'll consider it."

She smiled. "All right. I'll consider it," she replied, but did not know that she honesty would.

"Great. Are these the colors you decided upon?"

"I think so. I mean, I can always paint over it if I don't like them, right?"

"That's right. There are always second chances. You just have to take them."

The insinuation had not been lost on her, but she chose to ignore it. "Right, I mean it is just a wall."

"Come on. I will help you carry them to the check-out."

"Thank you. That is mighty kind of you."

When the cans were bought and paid for, he picked them up and helped her carry them to the old rusty pick up that she had borrowed from Mellie. He threw them in the back, and as she was about to thank him again, Rex appeared from around the corner.

His face said he was taken off guard, but he quickly covered it with the already familiar self-assured and cocky smirk.

"Well, well, what do we have here? It is a little soon for ya'll to be picking out paint colors together, but who am I to say. I don't waste time with the women I date either."

Kit cringed.

"I would use the word date loosely if I were you, Rex," Brady retorted childishly. "You've never lasted long enough with a woman to pick out paint colors."

Rex clamped his jaw shut and then said. "That's my choice and don't be jealous."

Brady started to respond, but Kit interrupted. "Brady just helped me carry them to the car."

Rex raised his hands in surrender. "Hey, teach, it's none of my business."

"Okay, well anyway. Thank you so much for your help, Brady, I appreciate it. I have got a lot of work to do, so I best get to it."

"It's no problem at all. Just remember not all of us guys are bad." He eyed Rex contemptuously.

Rex sniffed. "Yeah, I guess, some of us were raised right."

Brady shrugged. "Yeah, I guess so. Don't forget to contemplate my offer," he said, turning his attention back to Kit.

"I won't. Thanks gain." She quickly glanced at Rex, who was giving her a knowing look, and put the truck in reverse.

The last thing she wanted was to be caught in a brotherly rivalry, and it made a whole lot more sense after what Mellie had explained.

As she drove the narrow and windy roads back home, she doubted it even more that she would give Brady's invitation any more thought.

⚭⚭

He didn't know why he went there or even when he had made the decision to go, but when he was finished cleaning up at the bar, Rex found himself driving past his house and pulling up in front of hers.

He had not really expected for her to still be awake at that time of night or maybe she wouldn't even be home. She could have been shacked up at little brother Brady's house, for all he knew.

Needless to say, he was surprised to see her lights on. He slowed to a stop and turned off the engine. Before he could talk himself out of it, he was out of the truck.

Her windows were left slightly open, and he could hear music playing softly. Through the glow of the light, he could see her painting. He admired her worn jeans and tank top that were splattered with color, and he watched her toned arms and back muscles move under her smooth skin as she rolled the paint across the wall. Every so often, she would stop to work out a kink and to dance to the music.

She took a drink of her beer and sang along to a familiar ballad. He strained to hear her laughing softly, but was stunned into silence when the melody escaping her lips reached his ears. Damn, she was good. Like more than she might be able to carry a tune. She was really good.

Why did she continue to surprise him? He was bewildered, amazed, and pissed off all at the same time. Good God, did she get under his skin. He was about to walk away when she looked up and saw him through the window.

Kit met his eyes and held his stare. His legs carried him to her front door, and he walked through it. She stood there waiting for him to say something.

"What are you doing here?" she asked quietly.

Without hesitation, Rex crossed the small space separating them and grabbed her chin roughly and tilted it up toward his face. His mouth claimed hers with an audacity and force as if he was taking what was rightfully his.

Kit was so taken aback, at first she couldn't respond. Noticing this, he growled with frustration. He rolled his forehead across hers, and she could feel his breath on her face.

"Kit," he whispered. "Please."

She felt the hitch in her lower abdomen, and all her reservations left her body. It was replaced with unbridled want and need. She wrapped her arms around his neck and met his lips with vigor and enthusiasm. Their tongues intertwined and one hand grabbed her bottom, pulling her against him, while the other wrapped around the nape of her neck.

His fingers found her hair as his thumb caressed her cheek.

His hands were large and all over her. She moaned as she let go of all self-restraint, and she felt his appreciation.

When they came up for air, they were both left breathless and shaken.

"You really need to lock that door, don't you think?"

"Yes, probably," she whispered. "So can I ask, what are you doing here?"

"Honestly, I don't really know. I left work and, the next thing I knew, I was here. I apologize for showing up so late, but I wanted to check on you, make sure you were okay. So are you? Okay, I mean?"

"I think so. I was just having a painting party by myself."

Rex eyed her up and down. "I can see that."

Kit followed his gaze to her unruly appearance. "Oh, I must look a sight. I wasn't exactly planning on seeing anyone tonight?"

"So you were not planning on seeing my pain-in-the-ass so-called brother?"

"No, but why do you care?"

"I don't care. It's just a question."

"So you came to my house in the middle of the night partly to make sure I'm not with your brother whom you don't interact with. You manhandle me with intimate kisses, but you don't care. Okay, thanks a lot. It's all clear to me now," she said sarcastically.

"It is not like that."

She raised her eyebrows.

"Okay, it is like that. My apologies. Just the thought irritated the hell out of me. Reasonable? Probably not. Besides, I really did want to make sure you were okay."

"I appreciate that," she said honestly.

"And you were wrong about one thing."

"Oh yeah? What's that?"

"You're beautiful and far from a hot mess."

Her face resonated shock at first and turned to a sly grin. "Is there a softer side to Rex Jennings after all?"

Rex shook his head in annoyance. "Dammit, woman. You really do irritate the piss out of me."

"Yeah, yeah."

"So, how much more painting do you plan on doing tonight?"

"I'm hoping to finish this room."

"Do you need a hand?"

She eyed him suspiciously. "Most likely, as much as I need a hole in the head, but I'm going to accept against my better judgment."

"All right then."

He walked over to her table of supplies and picked up a roller, dipping it in the smooth pan of paint, making sure to evenly distribute the color, and began rolling it along the wall, careful to avoid the taped off edges.

She watched him for a moment in awe that this rough around edges man had shown up after his shift at Middy's, seemingly sober and was now helping her paint her living room. She did not dare try to figure out her feelings on the matter or what the aggressive kiss had meant.

In a short time, she had already come to realize that the more she tried to figure him out, the more confused she became. Maybe this was all because he had seen her with Brady and the other man had given him a verbal challenge that he was the better choice. Maybe it was all out of the competitive nature of their relationship that Mellie had spoken of, but she did not mention that as she was not supposed to know. Instead, she retreated to the refrigerator and uncapped another beer for him that she sat next to him, picked up her own roller, and began to work.

They worked in silence for a while, except for the music, in which she comfortably, but involuntarily hummed along to.

Rex enjoyed seeing her like this. In her own element and not so tightly wound. Hearing her hum along beautifully to the notes and being aware of her rhythmically brushing the paint with soft fluid motions, the quiet comforting sound of paint being applied to the wall lulled him to a zen state, and he was not sure the last time he had ever felt quite so at peace. Until he had it, he had not known how much he missed it or that he had been searching for it in all the wrong places all along.

Between the two of them, the work was done in half the time and, when the last square inch was finished, they stepped back to admire the finished product, simultaneously taking a drink of beer, rewarding themselves for all their efforts.

"It looks good. Looks like a lady lives here."

"Thanks. I'll take that as a compliment."

"No, really. It's a good choice on the colors. It really suits you."

"Thank you, Rex. For a moment there, you almost sounded…well, human, like you could care about something other than—"

"Getting drunk and getting laid? Thanks, occasionally I surprise even myself."

Kit smiled. "Yes, you can surprise."

"You surprise me too, you know. First impressions may not be all that they seem."

"Oh, and how do I surprise you?"

"Just everything. You have a lot of talents, and you're warmer than I expected. Maybe the ways of the South suit you."

"Maybe they do," she said quietly.

Their gazes held for a moment.

"I kind of have surprised myself too, you know. I know painting and fixing light fixtures is not only a man's job, but it was something Andy always took care of for me. Proving I can do some things on my own has been refreshing."

"Hey, not entirely on your own. Remember that, little missy. The favor will surely come back around some day," he joked.

"And I'll be happy to repay it."

"Oh, I'm sure you will." His eyes turned dark with desire and his meaning was evident, but he pushed it down to avoid her introverting herself once more. "But seriously, you're strong and should be proud of yourself."

Kit flushed.

"Why do you do that?"

"Do what?" she asked while turning to clean up.

"Get all uncomfortable at a compliment or turn away at any attention from a man? You're a young attractive woman. It can't be that you have had a lack of offers or experience."

She moved slowly and chose her words carefully. "I was with Andy for so long, we planned a future together, and then he was just gone, taken so suddenly. In my mind, I know that he isn't coming back, but my heart still feels like it's doing something wrong, like I'm dishonoring him or his memory and what we had. I think it takes a while to process that, and I'm still trying to catch up."

"I get that, I really do, but, Kit, Andy loved you. I'm sure of it, and because of that love, I'm sure he would want you to do whatever makes you happy."

"You speak the truth. I know that he would. I'm just still trying to figure out what it is that makes me happy."

Rex nodded. "You'll get there. It's part of the journey."

Kit looked up at him slowly.

"And are you there yet? Have you gotten to a place that makes you happy?"

Rex sighed. "I thought I had, but life has a way of changing, as you know. Admittedly I have been living a stagnant existence for some time."

"Do you think it's about time you start moving forward?"

"Probably. I reckon it is."

"I think your mom would want you to."

A realization passed over his face. "I know she would. For the first time in a long time, I think I want that, too."

Kit squeezed his hand. "Good."

Rex started to lean in, but Kit did not want to backtrack from the headway they had made. "Don't think so, Romeo. You do not get to sexualize this conversation. This was some ground-breaking stuff. It could have taken years of therapy for this kind of progress."

Rex groaned. "Have I ever told you that you irritate the piss out of me?"

"Once or twice. Now let's clean up. If you really want to help me, this is the least fun part of the job."

"You're a slave driver, teach, and have I mentioned the pay sucks?"

Kit laughed and gathered the tin buckets and cans to the sink, when out of the corner of his eye, Rex saw a flash of movement outside. He was out the door in an instant. "Stay put. If I'm not back in five, call the police."

CHAPTER 13

K it clutched her cell phone anxiously against her chest, nine-one-one already punched into the keypad, her thumb shaking over the send button. She pressed her face against the glass and strained to see.

Rex had bolted after someone or something that had caught his attention, and she had no idea if he was okay. Her palms were sweaty, and her heart beat in her chest, traveling up to her ears, drowning out any other sound than pounding drums.

He had said to call the police if he was not back in five minutes, and it seemed that time had stopped. She checked her phone every torturous second before she ventured out onto the porch.

"Rex?" she whispered loudly. "Rex? Are you okay? Are you out here?"

Leaves crunched in the near distance and Kit crept slowly toward the edge of the trees. She was shaking, but persisted forward.

Kit thought she saw a shadow of movement in the flow of the moonlight and she crouched behind a tree in an attempt to make herself invisible.

A branch broke somewhere too close for comfort,

and Kit put her hand over her mouth to stop herself from screaming. She tried to school her breathing to avoid being heard. Her body was trembling all over, and she looked around desperately for a sign of Rex. If something happened to him—

Suddenly, a large hand clamped down over her mouth while another grabbed her around her waist. She tried to scream, but no sound came out as the male hand was suctioned cupped around her mouth so tightly it muffled any sound she was able to get out. She bucked wildly against the force of the hold he had on her and tried desperately to pry his hand off of her mouth.

Her mind raced, and she tried to remember every defense strategy that Andy had ever taught her.

"Shhh, just stop, Kit."

The attacker knew her name.

He began dragging her toward the porch and she elbowed him hard in the ribs.

"Kit, it's me."

Then she heard a whoosh of air as she knocked the wind out of him.

"Shit, woman. What did you need me to protect you for?"

He released his hold on her, and she nearly collapsed to the ground before collecting her bearings.

"You don't listen worth a damn."

Kit whirled around to see Rex clutching his side, hunched over. "Rex!" she exclaimed, breathless, fear evident in her voice. "I thought you were him."

"I know what you thought," he muttered, still bent over. "And I thought I told you to stay put."

"I know, but I couldn't wait five full minutes before calling the police so I was trying to see—"

"If you could get us both killed?"

"No," she said defiantly. "I was trying to see if you

were okay or what was going on. Are you okay? I'm so sorry. What did you see? When you grabbed me, I thought I was being kidnapped. I was trying to fight for my life. Are you okay?"

"If you slow down for a minute, I'll answer you," he wheezed, still bent over. "I don't know who was out there, but I saw someone peeking in your window, and when I took off after him, the son of a bitch lost me. I damn near had him, too. Chased him until I lost his trail. I'm sure he's long gone by now, but he had no business being out here, of that I am certain."

"Oh, God," she said, covering her face with her hands. "Do you think it was him? The guy sending me the messages?"

Rex's lips were set in a hard line. "I think we can't rule out the possibility."

She sank to the ground in defeat and cried out, "What does he want from me? Why can't he just leave me alone?"

Rex gathered her in his arms and held her tightly, allowing her to cry. "It's okay. Let it all out. You're okay. I won't let anything happen to you, I promise you that."

"He was staring in my window. If this is all about Andy, he already took everything I have. Is that not enough?" she screamed in agony.

"I know, sweetheart. I know, but I'm here now. We're going to get him," he said soothingly, stroking her hair.

Just then a squad car came peeling around the corner, flinging loose gravel up as his tires tried to grab traction. The blue and red lights lit up her yard like a Christmas tree, but out of respect for the surrounding neighbors had not ran with sirens.

Brady jumped out of his car, hand on his gun.

"Rex, step away from the girl," he commanded.

"What? Are you going to shoot me now?" Rex asked sarcastically.

"Do as I say."

Rex sighed, but slowly obeyed, stepping away from Kit.

"Did someone here call nine-one-one?"

"I don't think so. I mean I was going to, but—" Kit reached in her pocket for her phone, coming up short. "I must have dropped it when you grabbed me," she said, looking at Rex.

"He grabbed you?" Brady asked." Are you hurt?" Looking at Rex, he yelled, "Keep your hands where I can see them."

Rex rolled his eyes, but obliged. "Just hold on a second, Deputy Dooey, and let the woman explain."

"Shut up, I want to hear it from her. And quit calling me Depute Dooey."

"He's right, Brady. He didn't hurt me, I swear. He saw a man watching us through the window, and Rex went out to chase him. He told me to stay put and to call the police if he didn't make it back. I dialed the number so that I'd be ready, but I didn't put the call through. When I couldn't see Rex, I went outside to investigate, and when Rex came back, he startled me, and I must have accidently dialed when I dropped my phone. I'm sure you'll find it over there by that row of trees. Rex was unable to catch him but chased him into the woods. We think it was probably the same person who's been leaving the morbid messages and newspaper articles about Andy."

"Is that right?" he said, looking at Rex.

"Yes, Deputy Dooey, I mean Officer Renshaw. Sorry, honest slip up; bad habit," Rex said about using the unflattering nickname. "Can I put my hands down now and can you point your laser beam elsewhere? My shoulders are going to be awfully sore after all the painting."

"That's why you were over here so late? You were helping paint?"

"Yes, what did you think I was doing?" Rex asked, raising his eyebrows.

Brady looked straight at Kit, his opinion obvious, but pride made him refuse to speak it out loud.

Kit winced, knowing he was miffed since he had offered to help her do the very same thing if only she had asked. "Rex showed up after work to make sure I was okay. He saw that I was painting by myself and offered to help," she explained. "It was really fortunate, actually, that he was here to see the peeper because who knows what would have happened had he not been here?"

"Yes, very fortunate indeed to have such a hands-on, helpful neighbor." Brady's voice held an edge that could not be denied.

"Well, some of us were taught to help our neighbors and how to treat a woman right. I guess it does come down to how you were raised." Rex wore a smug but hard smile.

"Now, wait just a minute, you pretentious little punk—"

"Boys, boys," Kit said, raising her voice and her hands. "Can we all just calm down and focus on the matter at hand? I'm not looking to be in the middle of some long historic sibling rivalry, nor am I a prize to be won, a victory to be celebrated to hang over the other's head. Am I the only one who sees the severity of the situation? Or is it just because I have the most to lose? Grow up. You two should be ashamed of yourselves."

"No, ma'am, I am very focused on the situation at hand, I promise you that," Brady apologized.

Rex smirked.

"I wouldn't be smiling, Mr. Jennings. My speech applied to you as well," Kit chastised him.

His smile slipped slightly. "Understood, teach."

"Now, let's go get my phone."

Brady unclipped his flashlight from his holster and started down the stairs.

"You're kind of cute when you're angry," Rex whispered behind her.

"You think so?" she asked, irritated. "Because there's plenty more where that came from."

"Looking forward to it."

"You're impossible," she said, shaking her head.

Brady shined his light at the leaves on the ground.

"I was standing right here," Kit said, and she knelt down, moving some of the leaves slightly. "Found it." She quickly glanced down at her call log. "Oh, I did place the call. I'm sorry. I hadn't realized."

"No need to apologize. I'm just glad you're okay. Do you have any idea who could have been out here tonight?"

She shook her head sadly. "No, I really don't, but I do know that it has to be connected. There's no way that this is all just a coincidence. I'm getting the feeling this is bigger than someone just leaving newspaper articles for me. Why would they come to my house in the middle of the night? Unless they wanted to scare me, or something worse?"

"I don't know, ma'am, but did this all start since you moved to Middle Bay or have you had previous altercations before moving?"

"I thought it started here, but the more I think about it, that just doesn't make sense. No one knows me here, and I haven't had a chance to make any enemies. While I was still in Watertown, I often felt like I was being watched or followed, but I had no real proof to back it up, and it was most logical to think that it was fear and my own mind playing tricks on me. It was partly why I decided to move and get a fresh start. Given the timing, I believe that someone followed me here and is trying to send a message or maybe finish what they started." Her voice cracked.

"Hey, now, we'll get to the bottom of this." Brady tried to reassure her, but he could not help but notice how she ever so slightly leaned toward Rex for support.

Kit wiped her nose with the back of her hand and tried to nod with confidence that she did not feel.

"We'll provide extra patrols, and I personally will be looking into it."

"Thank you," she sniffed.

"Do you want me to call Mellie?"

"No, I don't want to bother her at this time of night."

"That won't be necessary," Rex interjected. "I'm not leaving her alone. I'll sleep on the couch again tonight."

Kit did not argue because the thought of being alone terrified her.

Brady hesitated briefly, but seeing Rex concerned for someone other than himself was something Brady had not seen in a long while, since his mother, Julie, was sick. Given the small department that Brady worked for, they really could not afford to dispense an officer to shadow her twenty-four/seven, so reluctantly he had to agree that this was the best option.

Besides, he might think that Rex could be arrogant, sometimes nasty, and at times reckless, but when he cared for something or someone, he protected them fiercely, sometimes to a fault. It was evident that, for whatever reason, he had taken Kit under his wing, even if it was for his own personal interest. Brady trusted that he wouldn't let anything happen to her.

"Okay," he said, "well, that settles it for tonight, as

long as Ms. Harwick agrees."

"Yes, I would appreciate that." Her eyes were wide like saucers, and her voice took on a childlike quality. It was obvious she was weighed down by the overwhelming turn of events.

"Tomorrow, I plan to call Watertown PD to keep them abreast of the situation and see if they can give me further insight into what we're dealing with."

"Thank you. Ask for Sergeant Hunter. He can tell you everything."

"I'll do that," Brady said, jotting the name down in his notepad.

"Brady, you asked me when this all started, and looking back, I think it must have begun the night Andy was killed." She looked off into the night sky, staring, but not really seeing. "Honestly, maybe even before that."

"Okay, let's get you inside," Rex said as he grabbed her elbow and led her toward the door.

"Wait a minute." Brady stopped and pointed at a package left by the rusted porch swing. "Has that been here all night?"

"It's him," Kit said in a faint-hearted whisper. "That's what he was doing here. He was delivering me a message."

"Don't touch anything. I'll have it dusted for prints."

"I have to know what it says. Please," Kit begged.

Brady pulled out gloves and a pocket knife that he used to cleanly slice through the scotch tape. Inside, the make shift envelope was a sloppy hand written note. It was simple but none the less chilling.

He took everything from me and now it is payback.

"Oh, my gosh." Kit trembled. "Revenge for what? What could Andy have possibly done to deserve any of this?"

"I don't know, Kit, but the best news I have for you is that he's getting careless and that means it'll be all the more easy to catch him."

"That, or he truly has nothing left to lose." She shuddered. "He has made it this long, maybe he wants to get caught."

"No, not yet," Rex said.

"How do you know that?" she asked.

"Because he has not finished the job yet," he said solemnly. "What he wants is you."

The three of them stood in silence. No one argued what Rex said because, unfortunately, it was probably the truth.

Finally, Brady cut through the dramatic silence. "We have a plan of action. We'll send this to the lab for prints and run it past handwriting analysis. Kit, this guy will be behind bars, and you can put this nightmare behind you."

She nodded and squeezed her eyes shut. "I just desperately want to wake up."

Brady started to walk away, package in hand.

"Wait," Kit exclaimed. "Is there a picture in the shape of a puzzle piece?"

Brady looked at her in question.

"It comes with every package. I've kept them all."

She quickly retrieved them from the kitchen while Brady searched through the paper. When she returned, he was holding a single corner piece to the puzzle.

CHAPTER 14

It had taken Kit a long time to fall asleep, and the sun was coming up when she finally gave in to the overwhelming fatigue that took over her. Her eyes were grainy and puffy from all of the tears shed into her pillow when she awoke a couple of hours later.

Rex had listened to her sobs from the other room, knowing there was nothing he could say or do to make any of this any better. He was on the porch waiting for her when she finally ventured out.

Kit had done her best to make herself look presentable, but her eyes showed evidence of all the crying she had done.

"Did you make all that breakfast in there?" she asked.

"I didn't know what else to do," he said, shrugging off his kind gesture.

"So there is more to you than meets the eye."

"I'm full of surprises," he said half-heartedly.

"Did you even sleep at all?"

"Minimally," he lied.

"Well, I'm sorry to have dragged you into this mess. You didn't ask for it."

"What else do I have to do?"

"Probably enjoy life." She smiled. "You do not have to hang around."

"Like it or not, I'm in this," Rex said seriously. "I said I would stay with you, and I meant what I said. Believe it or not, Kit, I am a man of my word. I may not have a lot of integrity in your eyes, but my word is good for something."

"I'm realizing that, and you have more than you know," she admitted. "Hopefully, Brady finds out something soon, and we can all move past this. You can go back to your life of whatever it is that you do."

"Drinking beer and getting laid."

"That's not what I was thinking."

"Why? It's the truth."

Kit fell silent.

"Just let me help you and quit acting like you're a burden. If I didn't want to be here, I wouldn't be."

"Okay, fine then. Are you hungry? I'm sure you did not cook all that food for it to go to waste."

"No, I sure did not. You need to eat. You're too thin."

Kit looked down at her figure. "Okay, you did not have to wait on me to eat."

"Stop, just stop."

"Stop what, Rex? Why are you in a mood?"

"I'm not in a mood, but stop apologizing all the damn time. You have nothing to apologize for. You cannot help what's happening to you as much as I can't and stop treating me as if I'm a damn saint or a knight in shining armor because Lord knows that could not be further from the truth."

"Okay," she said quietly. "I just don't know why you are so mad at me."

Rex stood abruptly. "You listen to me." He grabbed

her face in his hands. "I'm not mad at you. That's not it at all, but damn right I'm angry. I'm angry that some psychopath is terrorizing you. I'm angry that he was so close and I couldn't stop him. I'm angry that he has hurt you before and is trying to hurt you again and there was nothing I could do about it. I feel helpless, and I hate that." He shook her ever so slightly before letting her go. "Don't you get that?"

"Yes, I get that," she whispered. "Are you angry that your mom got cancer, and even though you cared for her, it was not enough?"

"Damn right," he snapped. "And I'm angry that my piece of shit sperm donor left her to be a single mom, in order to raise another family. It does not bother me none, but her, she did not deserve that. She struggled being a single mom, when he had the means to make it better and chose not to. Back then, I did not want anything from him, or maybe I did, but secretly wanted him to want to, and if he did not want me, I did not want him. I was proud of her for not asking for anything, but when she got sick the first time, it was a real eye opener for me that at least his money could have helped her not be so stressed.

"When she got sick the second time…well, that was just pure hell, and I was old enough to know better and be really pissed. Should I let it go? Probably, but being angry is what fueled me some days. The blame had to go somewhere, and he was the easy target, especially when I saw Brady living the dream. So yeah, I guess to answer your question, I *am* pissed, but it's not at you, just at the injustice and unfairness of it all." He turned around and slammed his fist against his sides.

"I know," she whispered quietly, tears in her eyes. "I get it. Being helpless or powerless is just too much to bear sometimes."

"You know, I lay there last night, listening to you cry, and I knew that there was nothing I could do to help you. It reminded me of the past and my mom. It infuriated me for you and my mom, and if I'm being honest, it infuriated me for myself."

"I'm sorry to have reminded you," Kit said honestly. "That had to have been so hard."

"It was, it really was, but God, you have nothing to apologize for. I should be apologizing to you for being a selfish ass and unloading like this on you."

"One heartbreak does not have to outweigh or compete with another. One thing I have learned is that you can never control when the feelings and emotions arise. If it helps you to talk through it, then by all means, you should. Grief is a strange process. I never know what will trigger me or set me back, but you, virtually a complete stranger, have listened to me, and I want to be there for you. Everyone needs somebody, and as much as it's tempting to numb the pain, the answers are not going to be found at the bottom of a beer bottle or in the arms of bedmate after bedmate. The pain will always return until you work through it the hard way. But, gradually, it will get better or so I'm told anyway."

"How are you so wise and how have you remained compassionate?" he asked seriously.

"Oh, trust me, I have my moments where I'm not so wise."

"Like when you've responded to me physically?"

She blushed and avoided the question. "That's neither here nor there."

"Okay, we'll let that one go, but you should know that I try to be kind to women and always be upfront with my intentions or lack thereof. My mother taught me that much, but I don't always tend to respect them. Kit, you're big hearted and infuriating as hell, but I respect you, even when I don't show it."

Kit was taken aback his candor and it showed. "Thank you, Rex. Since you said that, I just want to throw this out there. You can take it or leave it, but for what it's worth, you have every right to be angry with your father, but Brady did not have a choice as much as you did not. Maybe now that you all are adults and out of the nest, you could work on coexisting in the future because neither of you had control over the past. Just some food for thought."

Rex remained silent for some time. "Okay, I'll chew on it and let you know how it turns out. Speaking of food, our is getting cold. We'd best be getting to it."

∽∾∽∾

Last night had been close, too close. He had let himself get caught up in the moment, and it had almost cost him everything he had painstakingly worked for. Wouldn't it have been something if he had walked free for almost a year after killing a cop only to be caught now before his work was completed?

He had promised himself he would remain clear headed and keep his head down until he executed his plan, but he had let himself have a few too many last night, and he got sloppy. He could not afford to make that mistake, especially when he was so close to the end.

All the ground work, stakeouts, and late nights would have been for nothing. Revenge had been the only thing on his mind for nearly two years, and he would be damned if he didn't get it. He knew that the alcohol changed him. He was not in denial about that, but dammit if a man did not deserve a little liquid courage now and again.

Watching her had been a thrill, a feeling he had not felt in a long time. Invading her privacy, being there when she thought she was all alone.

He had studied Officer Anderson Slade from the moment he had his first encounter with him, and when things had really gone south, his need to know everything about Slade could have been called an obsession by some, but he knew better. Knowledge was power, and everyone had a weak point. You just had to find it. Slade had taken everything away from him. When he had begged and pleaded, the officer had shown him no mercy. The prick thought he was better than him, and he knew he was going to show him differently.

As luck would have it, through his surveillance, he learned that Slade had a cute little fiancée waiting at home. It could not have been more perfect. An eye for an eye was his philosophy, so he had begun adding Kit Harwick to his studies until he knew her and her routine better than she knew herself. He had eyes on her anytime he reasonably could.

He went through her trash, collected her receipts. He knew that she was writing a novel and even got to read many of the pages she had thrown out.

Once, he even followed her when she was dropping off old clothing to the local charity. He had hit the jackpot when he was able to go through the bags before they were taken inside. He allowed himself to take a few personal belongings, even some feminine articles of clothing—a bra or two. Lace, she liked like, and so did he, but she had expensive tastes for being merely a teacher and surviving on a cop's salary.

He could recall the smell of her perfume and, man, did it smell nice. He wished his old lady could have smelled that nice.

Once, when he was on a stakeout, knowing Slade

was on the beat, Kit had left the house suddenly, forgetting to lock the door behind her. He knew it was risky, but he could not resist. He allowed himself to go in and admire all of their things. He was careful not to touch too much. He was not that stupid, but in her haste, she forgot to wear her engagement ring and left it on the bathroom counter.

He thought he had hit the jackpot and even contemplated pawning it just for shits and grins, but it occurred to him that Slade being a cop and all could eventually track down where the ring went, and he did not want it to be traced back to him.

So he merely moved it. He put it in a coffee mug, knowing they would eventually find it. All cops drank coffee, right? But in the meantime, he would have fun watching her squirm, turning the house upside down looking for it.

Maybe she wouldn't tell Slade or maybe she would. Oh, the joy he would have felt if Andy boy came unglued. Kit would swear, "I left it on the counter like I always do."

Slade would yell how she should have kept something so valuable in a much safer place.

He almost giggled to himself now as he remembered the excitement. For days he watched her idly reach for the third finger on her left hand, but in less than a week the shiny rock was put back proudly on display, disappointing him only mildly, for he knew worse was yet to come.

He knew they were pregnant before Slade did. He saw the multiple boxes in the trash. If it was negative, she would have only taken one. Seeing as how they were not married yet, one could safely assume this "by the book" couple was not actively trying.

Then one day, he overheard her on the phone, presumably with the doctor's office. She was on her way out the door, but he heard her exclaim. "So I'm pregnant? I'm really pregnant." After a brief pause she said, "I would like to make an appointment right away."

She was crying, maybe out of shock and disbelief, but the sound of her voice could not be mistaken. She was happy, overjoyed even, and that grated his nerves. How dare they start a family when they had screwed up his?

That was when he knew he had to act fast. He was going to put an end to their happiness if it was the last thing he did.

Up until recently, he had been executing it perfectly, if he did say so himself, but he had not counted on her moving. That was a huge hitch in his plan, and he had merely weeks to prepare. That had not been easy with his limited funds, but he had not been about to quit now.

Since then, it had been one challenge after another and all seemed to revolve around her neighbor Rex Jennings. Man, that guy was a pain in his ass, and that little hussy had not even waited a full year before allowing someone else to warm her bed.

Rex almost got to him last night, and it was surprising Rex hadn't caught him with the buzz he had going. Lucky for him, it was dark. Otherwise, he would not be sitting here a free man, but Lord if the knot on his head that he had acquired from hitting a low hanging branch had not nearly knocked him out.

That combined with a nasty hangover had his head pounding this morning. He thought a million little drummer boys were having band practice on the inside of his skull.

Lisa hugged impatiently. "I thought we were going to make a move by now. Incite a lover's quarrel between those two or something." She took a long drag off of her cigarette. "What is taking so long?" she whined.

"Don't get your panties in a twist, darling, and I bet they're cute little panties, they are." He grinned and she squirmed away from him uncomfortably. "Good things come to those who wait," he said.

"Oh, yeah…well, what are we going to do now?"

"We're going to bite the dog that bit me last night and go get a stiff drink. Then we will do a little recon."

CHAPTER 15

S o are you going to be okay going to work?"

"Yes, Rex. I'm grateful that you're concerned, but I cannot call in to a job I just started, and I highly doubt that he's going to come after me in such a public place. Besides, I know that you have already given the details to MJ and the director so they're going to be on extra high alert."

"Fine, but I switched my shift at Middy's from the night shift to brunch, and I'll get off sometime early evening. If you need anything at all, I want you to call me."

"I will, but won't you be taking a pay cut not working the late night?"

"Seriously?" He eyed her questionably. "This is the south, sweetheart, people start drinking right after work, and some around these parts find it acceptable to take their whiskey with breakfast. Not to mention, I'll get plenty of tips with the dinner crowd. No worries, but I mean it. I want you to call me immediately if anything happens out of the ordinary."

"I got it boss. I'll call if Billy picks his nose or if Johnny gets in trouble for spitting, you'll be the first to know about it." She smiled a cheesy smile his way.

"Hey now, little lady. There's no need for sarcasm or you'll be the one sent home with a progress report."

"Whoa, I'm scared."

"You should be or I'll be forced to punish you." He licked his lips invitingly.

Kit flushed and swatted his arm. "I got the message loud and clear."

"Good, now try and have a good day at work."

"You too, dear," she yelled as she hopped up into the driver's seat of the old Chevy.

When she arrived at work, she was relieved to be doing something that was her normal routine. She was back in the world of the living, and it felt good. She even enjoyed breaking up playground arguments, wiping noses, and consoling heated temper tantrums. It was something she was good at, and it made her feel needed.

"You look awfully happy for someone that has a psychopath sending her messages," MJ remarked.

Kit took a deep breath. "I have my moments, but it feels good to be at work. I feel normal."

"Good, but honestly, are you okay? How are you holding up?"

"Obviously, I could be better, but I'm really trying to trust that the police have it under control, and this lunatic will be behind bars soon. If it means justice for Andy, then I will take the good with the bad, I suppose."

"You're stronger than me," MJ said.

"Girl, I highly doubt that. I saw how many tequila shots you drank the last time we went out. You can hold your own."

MJ laughed. "Well, you still have your sense of humor and that alone amazes me."

"I'm lucky to have found a good support system in such a new place. That helps. Don't get me wrong, we had friends in Watertown. Andy was liked and respected by almost everyone, but most of them were part of the police family. It was just too close to home after he died. For them and me. For me, it reminded me of what I no longer had and, for them, I think I served as a constant reminder of what could happen to any of them on any given day. Not to mention, I lost my future husband, but they also lost a brother in blue, number two thirty-seven." Kit shook her head. "It was hard for everyone, and I understood, but I also know that, at any given time, if I needed anything, they would be there for me. Once you are a part of the family, you're in it to stay, and I find comfort in that."

"What about your blood family? Like your mom and dad? Do you miss them?"

"What is blood really?" Kit asked. "I'm an only child and, although my parent's address reads from Watertown, they're not really there much. They travel, in the pursuit of happiness, chasing their dreams."

"Sounds magical."

"It's not, trust me. They won't find what they're looking for. They're two very unsatisfied people. That's why they left Middle Bay so long ago, and I would like to say they found what they were looking for, but I'd be lying. Mom got pregnant with me when she was just a kid herself. Dad married her because it was the right thing to do." Kit shrugged. "I don't know how much love was involved back then, but it certainly was not the forever kind of love you dream about as a child. Unfortunately, neither believed in divorce or at least the families they came from did not, but they also did not believe in counseling or airing their dirty laundry so their relationship never got better.

"When I lived with them, I remember being able to actually feel the bitterness and resentment, and it was not kept secret that I was the reason they had to stay together. It's sad, really, to be that miserable, lonely, but neither of them ever tried to make it better. There have been a lot of affairs on both sides of the equation, and they are both guilty of constantly trying to make themselves happy without a care or any disregard for the other.

"They somehow manage to look like they have it together, by traveling and buying all the latest things, but I don't know who they think they're fooling. Everyone knows. In a small town, word gets around, as I'm sure you are well acquainted with. Middle Bay is considered an ant, compared to Watertown, the breadcrumb on the map. They're not horrible people, just calloused and cold." Kit sighed. "So to answer your question, they stood by my side when Andy was laid to rest but were on a flight the next day, flying to Vegas because Dad had a free weekend from hitting it big on the black jack tables. I don't think they can fathom what I was going through, losing the love of my life."

"Gosh, I'm sorry," MJ breathed. "My parents are the complete opposite, could not rub two pennies together to make a dime, but they loved fiercely with all of their hearts. It makes me think how lucky I really was."

"You were." Kit smiled wistfully. "But don't feel sorry for me. Instead of falling into the trap of cold despair, I learned very early that I had the perfect example of what not to be like. I was very fortunate. Andy and I had more love and happiness in our short time together than they will ever have if they live to be old and gray. Mellie, on the other hand, I'm not sure how she gave birth to my mother. She has shown me more love and support than I could ask for. She's a true nurturer."

"You must get it from her then, Kit Harwick, because you're a remarkable person, and I am glad to call you a friend."

"And I, you, Mary Jane. It's because of people like you that I still have my faith in humanity."

The girls shared a tear-filled hug before MJ pulled away."

"So you can tell me to mind my own business or go straight to hell if you want."

"I would never."

"Okay, good. Do you believe in only one love of your life?"

Kit hesitated.

"Because I do not, and you're so young so I don't want you to think your opportunity for happiness is gone."

"I would like to think there is more in store for me, at some point, but I'm just not sure if I'm at a place where I can answer that yet."

"I guess what I am trying to say is that sometimes your second chance comes around when you least expect it, and I do not want you to shut it down because you have something in your head about time restrictions. Andy sounds like he was a wonderful man, and I'm sure he would want you to be happy."

"Of that I have no doubt. It's in my own head that the struggle exists, but Andy would want me to pursue whatever made me happy, of that I am certain. If and when that time comes around, I hope I'm not too jaded to see it."

"Well it may be staring you right in the face."

"What are you saying? Rex?" Kit exclaimed. "You cannot be serious?"

"Maybe." MJ shrugged. "You have been spending an awful lot of time together, and you both have experienced heartache and loss."

"Rex has been helping me out, which I admit goes against my earliest assumptions of him, but settling down isn't exactly his MO. I'm not sure we are either of the other's type."

"Maybe opposites do attract. You cannot say there have not been sparks between the two of you."

Kit thought back to all of their close encounters and shook her head defiantly. "We're just stuck together in the middle of chaos right now, that's all."

"I'm just asking you to try and be open. Consider the possibilities and if I'm wrong, I will say I am wrong. Deal?" MJ stuck out her hand.

"Fine, but I'm telling you, you're wrong."

"Maybe so, but I would not be a friend if I did not call it like I see it."

"Geez, friend, you sure do have the worst timing."

MJ smiled. "Sometimes that's how life works. It gives us a swift kick in the rear."

"Ain't that the truth."

෬෬

At lunch, Kit checked her phone and was surprised to see a voicemail from Sergeant Jacob Hunter. Seeing the familiar name and knowing the reason he was calling gave her a sudden pang of sadness.

She listened to it carefully.

"Kit, hey it's Jay. I was calling to check up on you. I know it has been a while. I received a call from Officer Brady Renshaw regarding the messages you have been receiving." There was a long pause on his end. "Kit, you know you should have called me. It tears me up, what you're going through. Anyway, he faxed over copies of all of the evidence, and we have major case checking into it and analyzing the handwriting. We're going to get him for you and for Slade. We're also checking into any disgruntled citizens that Slade may have come into contact with, so hang tight and know that we're on this. If you could give me a call back, and, Kit, stay safe, be smart. You have a lot of people looking out for you. One more thing, Watertown is holding a memorial November first in honor of the anniversary of Andy. You should be there. We would all love to see you. If I did not say it already, stay safe, and talk to you soon."

Kit's eyes filled with tears as she listened to the message again. A memorial in Watertown. She suspected they would hold some kind of event in remembrance of their fallen officer, and she knew without having to think it through that she would be there, no matter what, but the emotions that came over her were stifling and paralyzing.

She longed to talk to Hunter, but she could not call him back now. She would never make it through the rest of her day. It would have to wait until she was alone and could truly break down and crumble.

"Go home, sweetie," the director said behind her. "You've been through so much. MJ and I can handle the rest of the day. Take all the time you need. Your job will be here."

"I could not possibly."

"I insist. Go be with Mellie and take care of yourself."

Kit thanked her before walking out the door.

So much for normal, she thought.

∽∾∽

This was it, Lisa thought as she stood on Rex's front stoop. She was going to give it everything she had, and if Rex denied her, then he must really be a Neanderthal. She went through a lot of trouble for him, even got a bikini wax, and that shit was painful. He better be worth it.

She knocked on the door and placed her best "come take me now" look on her face.

Rex answered the door, and she was reminded of how long it had been. She hoped he remembered.

"Lisa, what are you doing here?" He looked perplexed.

"Hey, lover," she purred.

He eyed her skeptically. "Hey, I'm on a lunch break from Middy's. I took an earlier shift, and I have to head back shortly. What's up?"

"This won't take long. Can I come in?" She smiled at him tantalizingly.

"I was about to head out, like I said."

"Oh, come on, Rex, no time for an old friend?"

She twisted the straps of her trench coat coyly and shifted her weight from one wedged foot to another, revealing a lot of thigh as she tossed her hair.

Against his better judgment, he opened the door farther to let her through. "Okay, but I'm on a time crunch so I have really got to make this fast."

She sauntered into the cabin. "Lucky for me, fast is just the way I like it."

∽∾∽

Kit decided to run home to grab a few things before heading to Mellie's where she would wait for Rex to call whenever he got off.

As she turned down the gravel road it occurred to her that she had not called him to let him know she had gotten off work early.

It felt strange depending on a man again, and she found herself wishing the circumstances could be different.

Damn MJ for filling her mind with needless nonsense. She could not afford to be thinking about these things.

She was sure that Rex simply saw her as he did every woman, a challenge, but she would be lying to herself if she said she had not enjoyed the attention and occasional flirting. It let her know that on some level she was still a viable living breathing female with some sex appeal. It reminded her that she was alive and that was in its own way nice.

When she rounded the corner she saw Rex's truck in the driveway and a small spark of pleasure filled her. Home on lunch, she guessed. She could just stop in and inform him of her plans now, and he wouldn't be angry that she hadn't called.

She pulled in behind him and walked up the stoop. She knocked once before, turning the handle to let herself in.

"Hey, I was in the neighborhood and—"

She stopped short at the sight before her.

Lisa. The blonde from the bar, and all of her naked glory. Brazilian wax and all standing over Rex where he was seated on the couch.

Lisa wore a smug smile, and Rex wore a look a surprise.

"I'm sorry to interrupt. I'm leaving," Kit said abruptly and slammed the door shut behind her. "Oh, my God. Oh my God. Oh my God," she muttered all the way to the truck.

"Kit, wait," Rex yelled.

"No, I don't think I will," she said, grabbing the door handle.

He hopped the steps and came up behind her, covering her hand.

"It's not what it looks like, I swear."

"Really, because it looks like your old screw buddy met you on your lunch break for a quickie."

"Okay," He sighed reluctantly. "That is apparently why she's here, but I came home for a simple sandwich. I had no idea that she was going to show up unannounced like this."

"You know what? I—It's really none of my business," Kit stammered. "I came to tell you they let me off early, and now you know. I won't be needing further assistance and I am sorry to have gotten in the way this much."

"Kit, don't do that. I want to be there for you, don't shut me out."

"It looks to me like you are rather busy. You shouldn't keep a girl waiting. It's rude, so I'll let you get back to it."

"I don't have feelings for Lisa. I didn't want her here, please don't go like this. Come in and let's talk about this."

"I don't know how they do things in the South, but where I come from, three is a crowd."

"And that's not what he said earlier."

They both looked up to the porch where Lisa stood with her trench coat loosely tied.

"That stuff about not having feelings or wanting me here. His body said otherwise, if you know what I mean so I would say one of us is getting played."

"Yeah, I know exactly what you mean, Lisa, and I would say he's trying to play us both. You don't have to worry about me. I'm out."

Kit boosted herself into the truck, and Lisa stood there like the winner of the local sportsman's club turkey shoot, proud of her accomplishment and enjoying the fight escalating before her eyes.

"Don't listen to her, Kit, it's all horse shit. Where are

you going? You can't be alone," he screamed as she pulled down the drive.

The window was open and after she squealed the tires she paused. "What I do is no longer your concern, but seeing as how I know no one in this God-forsaken mosquito-infested town I'll be at Mellie's. If she is really spewing horse shit, then you can eat shit for all I care. No offense to you, Lisa."

"None taken." Lisa smiled and waved her hand.

"And one more thing." Kit slowed the down. "You are most definitely not my second-chance soul mate, not that I ever thought you were, but others might have, and this just confirms they couldn't have been more wrong."

"W—What?" Rex sputtered, trying to catch her.

Kit peeled away back in the direction that she had come.

"Kit, dammit." Rex kicked dust as he watched her drive away.

享享享

Kit was fuming as she drove too fast for the country roads.

"That no good son of a bitch," she said aloud, as she fishtailed around a corner.

She needed to calm down driving these still unfamiliar roads. She needed to get up to Mellie's house in one piece.

She wouldn't give her stalker the satisfaction of wrapping herself around a tree or hurting someone else, for that matter.

When she was close to Mellie's, she pulled off to the side of the road to compose herself. Her grandmother did not need to see her in distress and when she pulled down the visor she was confronted by a mascara-smeared reflection. She did her best to wipe the residue from under her eyes, but Mellie would be too astute not to notice her granddaughter's apparent emotional breakdown.

Kit did not know why she cared so much about Rex's actions. He owed her nothing, but she was under the impression he was trying to run over a new leaf, and she'd believed him when he was kind to her. What a fool she had been. It was all part of the game, and she had been too wrapped up in what was going on around them to realize.

She was disappointed, and what was more confusing was why. She flipped the visor up, put the truck in drive, looked through the windshield, and noticed a cloud of smoke.

No, it was more than a cloud, it was billowing black smoke up being projected upward, filling the surrounding air.

"Oh, my word," she exclaimed as dread washed over her.

It was coming from the direction of Mellie's house. She drove onward and soon saw orange flames flickering in the distance.

ぐろくろ

When his pager went off, Rex could not have been in a worse mood to go fight a fire, but when the address came across the screen, he had never moved faster.

"Dammit, Kit," he cursed as he ran to his truck. It was becoming a familiar phrase. He called the department on his way. "Send the largest truck we've got to the plantation. Be advised I'm heading straight to the scene."

CHAPTER 16

When Rex pulled up to the house, the entire left wing was engulfed in flames, and his heart was pounding when he saw Kit's truck parked outside. He jumped out and ran toward the house quickly, yelling as he went. "Mellie? Kit? Are you in there?"

He checked the front door and found that it was locked. He took a step back and could see flames through the window.

He ran as fast his legs could carry him to the side entrance that almost all invited guests used. It led into the kitchen and, although the door handle was warm to the touch, it was unlocked, and he used his shirt sleeve as a heat protectant and was able to push it open.

The room was full of black smoke and the heat was overwhelming.

"Mellie? Kit? Can you hear me?"

After no response, he dropped to his knees and covered his mouth and nose with the neck of his shirt to avoid excess smoke inhalation. He army-crawled across the floor to the hallway and, although the smoke was still thick, he was relieved to see that it was a little more clear, and he could get a better visual. It had been sometime since he had been in the house, and he was a little disoriented on the layout.

His training told him that the fire had probably started in the direction that he had come from and, although it was intense, it had not been going long.

Rex was able to crouch to a low walking position which allowed him to move faster. He knew time was of the essence if they wanted to preserve the rest of the house.

"Mellie, Kit, can you hear me?" he called out.

"In here."

Hearing a muffled cry, he recognized Kit's voice and said a silent prayer of gratitude as he hurried in her direction, rounding the corner toward a laundry room.

"Rex. We're in here, please hurry."

He shouldered the door open with a forceful shove, and his body weight propelled him into the room. It was quickly filling with smoke, and small flames licked the interior wall as the fire traveled in toward the center of the house.

Kit had opened a window in an attempt to get fresh air as they planned an escape.

Mellie was laying on the ground as Kit pleaded with her to get up.

"Rex, Mellie's hurt. It's her leg. I can't move her," she exclaimed. "'The shelving must have collapsed, and it's heavy."

"Okay, all right. Let's remain calm. I'm going to get you out of here. Mellie, are you with me?"

"Yes," the older woman moaned.

"Is she going to be okay?" Kit pleaded.

"Mellie, do you know who I am?"

"Of course, Rex, my leg is hurt. I'm not dead."

Rex looked at Kit. "She's going to be just fine, but I'm going to need your help in moving her."

Kit's eyes were wide and she nodded agreeably.

"I want you to stabilize her head and keep talking to her while I move the boards. The ambulance and fire department are on their way, but we need to be careful that she does not have internal injuries."

Kit got down beside Mellie and cradled her head between her hands. "I'm right here, Mellie. Rex is going to help us. He's going to get us out of here, stay with me."

Rex analyzed the position of the shelf and Mellie's wounded leg. After determining that a major artery did not appear to be damaged, he stood up, holding his breath, and took off his belt.

"What are you doing?"

"This is probably unnecessary, from what I can see, but I want you to use this as a tourniquet to prevent any major blood loss. Right now the weight of the shelves are providing enough pressure, but when I move them, there will be a release of that pressure. I want you to immediately wrap this around her thigh and squeeze as tight as you can. Do you understand?"

Kit nodded silently.

"Once I have the debris out of the way, we can determine the best way to move her. Are we all on the same page?"

"Yes."

Rex was sweating bullets as the heat grew closer to them. They had to act fast. "Mellie are you still with me?"

The woman groaned in response.

"Okay, that's my girl." He wiped his hands on his pants leg to make sure he could get a good grip. "Okay, ready? On the count of three. One, two, three, go."

He pushed with super-human strength and was able to unpin the woman from an almost certain death trap. He hoisted the shelving unit awkwardly while Kit scurried beneath him to tie the belt around Mellie's leg. "Have you got it?" he grunted.

"I got it. Rex, there's blood."

"Is it squirting?'

"No, just pooling slightly."

"Okay, that's okay. Mellie, are you with us?"

The woman moaned in pain.

"I'll take that as a yes. Okay now, Kit, I want you to roll Mellie as carefully as possible out of the way so that I can move these shelves away from her without blocking the door. We may need that as an exit strategy. Can you do that?"

Kit nodded.

Rex's arms were shaking from the weight of the boards, but he did not let it show. "Okay, I'm going to count to three again and then roll her toward the washer and dryer."

He counted and Kit moved Mellie while the woman yelped in pain. When it was clear, Rex dropped the boards and knelt beside them, gulping fresh air. He could hear the sirens approaching even over the sound of the smoke detectors blaring in his ear. He checked the woman's pulse and was relieved to find it was steady beneath his touch.

"Okay, she's stable for now so. Kit, I'm going to need you to be strong because we need to get her out of here. This house is confusing if you've never been in it so I'm going to hoist you through the window, and you're going to meet the trucks to tell them where we are."

"I'm not leaving her." Kit shook her head in vain.

"Kit, listen to me. The best thing you can do for Mellie is to get help quickly. There's no way, in her condition, that she can get out through the window without risking further damage. I'll stay with her, applying pressure, but we're going to need to stabilize her on a stretcher to get her to a hospital. Can you help me help her?"

Kit's face was tear filled and streaked with soot, and she hiccupped as she agreed. "Okay, hang on Mellie, help is on the way."

Rex stood and cupped his hands to give Kit a boost through the small window. There was broken glass, and he grabbed a dirty linen to best cover the shards and avoid injuring Kit in her departure.

Kit put her foot in his hold and he whispered, "I won't let anything happen to her. Now go, you can do it."

He pushed her up and out, and Kit squeezed through the limited space.

When she was out the window, she ran, gulping in clean air, and when she rounded the side of the house, emergency vehicles were waiting.

"They're in the laundry room, down the hall from the kitchen, second door on your right. Hurry, Rex is in there with my grandmother. She's hurt, bleeding from her leg, and they're running out of air. Rex said you need a stretcher and oxygen waiting."

The chief of the fire department, they had appropriately named Yogi, stood yelling out orders. "You heard the lady, now go."

Men threw on their helmets and ran toward the blaze while the others uncoiled their hose, ready to distinguish the angry flames.

Medics rushed her, asking if she was okay, begging for her to sit in the back of the ambulance to be evaluated, but she refused, insisting that she would get checked out when she knew her grandmother was okay.

Her adrenaline was pumping too much for her to sit down now. Moments passed that felt like an eternity before men in their bunker gear emerged from the house carrying a stretcher with Mellie strapped to it. Kit's heart leapt. They made it, her grandmother was out, but then her eyes searched frantically before relief filled her. Rex followed them out, slick with sweat and covered in soot, his eyes squinting in the descending sunlight.

Kit ran toward the stretcher. "I'm right here, Mellie. It's going to be okay. You're safe now."

"Ma'am, we need to get her to the truck, but we'll keep you updated. Just give us some space."

Kit backed away and held her hands to her face as she watched them put a mask on and take Mellie's vitals.

When she looked back over Rex was adorned in full protectant gear and was shouting to his team.

He met her eyes, and she said a million words without speaking.

"Thank you," she mouthed to him and he nodded solemnly as a medic led her away to administer oxygen.

After determining Kit's injuries were minor and mostly superficial, they let her rejoin Mellie in the back of the ambulance. Before it took off for the hospital, Brady ran toward her.

"I know you have to go, but there's something I thought you should see."

Kit leaned out of the back of the ambulance. "Now?"

"Yes, now."

He held a familiar looking handmade envelope, and her heart sank. She opened it quickly. Her hands were trembling and dirty as she read.

An eye for an eye. He took away my family, now I take yours. A person shows their true colors when the temperature rises.

Sure enough, beside it was yet another puzzle piece.

CHAPTER 17

K it emerged from the hospital room, hours later, tired and emotionally drained. She was still dirty, and the smell of the smoke clinging to her made her sick to her stomach.

She had waited restlessly while the doctors tended to Mellie. When they finally emerged, she was greeted by a doctor. His scrubs were splattered with blood.

It brought her back to almost a year before when she sat in a very similar situation and the prognosis had changed her life forever.

This time, she was alone and had nothing but time to remind herself that what happened to Mellie was all her fault. If she didn't have a crazed stalker, Mellie would be enjoying the simple things in life rather than being treated in a hospital bed. When she saw the blood on the doctor, she thought she would nearly faint. He removed his scrub cap, and Kit's knees went weak.

"Mellie lost some blood, but we replaced it. She's stable and resting comfortably. She had to have some stitches which may leave a lasting scar, given her age. We're treating her for smoke inhalation, but expect that she'll make a full recovery."

Kit expelled a breath of relief. "Oh, thank God."

"Yes, indeed," the doctor agreed. "It's a miracle that she's even alive, given the circumstances, but it could have been much worse. She should heal quickly and return to normal soon. For the time being, we've got her on some pretty heavy pain killers to help her sleep and keep her comfortable. You can see her now, but just be aware she'll probably be pretty groggy."

"Oh, thank you, Doctor. This is such a relief to hear."

Kit hung out with Mellie for most of the night, watching her sleep, and talking quietly for the few moments when she would wake.

"Mellie, I am so sorry. This is all my fault. I hope that someday you'll find it in your heart to forgive me. I would never have put you in harm's way if I had known how far he would go," Kit cried to the sleeping woman.

Mellie opened one eye. "Sweet child. This is no fault of yours. You can't control someone else's actions. You have to learn to forgive yourself because you do not need forgiveness from me."

"So you know? About the messages?"

"I've talked to Brady. Small town, my dear, you'll learn eventually. Nothing's secret around these parts. Just promise me that you'll be safe."

"I will, Mellie. Thank you for your mercy."

"Oh, please, don't thank me. Just listen to me. You let the police handle their job, and you have constant protection until that lunatic is caught. That Rex Jennings seems like a good choice to me." Mellie closed her eyes, but a smile played on her pale lips.

"Oh, Mellie, I promise to be careful, but I don't think that Rex is a good choice."

"A good choice for what?" Rex asked from the doorway.

He had cleaned up moderately, but it was obvious he had come straight from the scene and had merely changed his clothes. He held a bouquet of store bought flowers that he sat on her night stand.

"Well, thank you, Rex. They're lovely. We were just discussing how you would be a good choice to watch out for my dear Kit here."

"Ma'am, I've tried, and I'll respect your wishes and continue to do so, if she'll let me."

"Oh, she'll let you, because she won't go against her grandmother's wishes while she's lying in a hospital bed."

Kit eyed her suspiciously. "Oh, you're good, Mellie. I'll give you that. What are you up to?"

"Oh, just finding you a new beau. Isn't my granddaughter beautiful?"

"Don't listen to her. She's on drugs," Kit said hastily.

"Yes, Mellie, she's very beautiful." Rex held Kit's gaze as Mellie smiled groggily.

"Rex is a busy man, though, Mellie," Kit countered. "I could not possibly expect him to take time out of his busy schedule for me."

"I'm not as busy as you think. Sometimes appearances can be deceiving. Besides, if you think that I'm letting you out of my sight after today, you're sadly mistaken. I've never been so scared," he said seriously.

"Oh, you two, go kiss and makeup," Mellie interjected.

"Mellie," Kit exclaimed, embarrassed.

"Oh, leave her be," Rex said. "Aren't there worse things than letting her have a little fun playing match maker?"

"Rex? How's my house? Were you able to save it?" Mellie asked.

"Ma'am, I did my best. It'll need to be investigated for structural damage, but with your homeowner's insurance, it should be able to be restored with a complete kitchen remodel. Most of the damage was confined to that area of the house. The rest was virtually unscathed."

"Thank heavens."

"I thought you'd be happy to hear that."

"No, son, I'm talking about the kitchen. I've been thinking it needed to be updated, but I didn't want to spend the money," she joked.

"I see where you get your perseverance from," Rex said to Kit.

Kit remained silent, just watching her grandmother rest.

"Kit?"

"Yes, Mellie?"

"Are you going to stay here and watch me sleep all night?"

"I planned on it."

"Please don't. I really just want to rest, and you need yours too. Not to mention, you need to get this stalker off of the streets and plan your trip for the memorial."

"How did you know?"

"I know all."

"You talked to MJ, didn't you?"

"Maybe, but even so, I'm going to take my next pill and drift off into La, La Land. I want you to leave with Rex and sleep or don't sleep—either way, it's none of my business."

"Mellie, now, I know it's the drugs talking.'

'Rex, take her out of here."

"Yes, ma'am."

Kit reluctantly kissed Mellie's forehead and advised the night nurse to call with any changes. When they were alone in the hallway, Kit shuffled her feet awkwardly.

"So, are you ready to go?" Rex asked hopefully.

"Look, I'm so grateful for everything you did for Mellie and for me. You saved our lives and kept us all calm. I don't want to think about what would have happened had you not been there. I'm thankful, relieved, impressed by you, but we don't really have to do this."

"Do what?"

"Pretend like you want to take on this chore of looking after me."

They stood in front of the elevators, and Rex turned her to face him before pushing the button.

"Listen closely," he said, grabbing her waste. "I know you were upset with me earlier."

"Rex, I can hardly be mad at you after your heroic actions this afternoon, but you don't have to play roles of both hero and romantic interest."

"Kit, one thing has nothing to do with the other. You have every right to be upset, but what you saw was just bad timing. I don't know what Lisa was up to, but it certainly was not invited by me. Maybe she was jealous and felt threatened by you, as well she should, but I was just as surprised by her actions as you were and, believe me, when I say I was turning her away and she knew it. No matter how bad it looked."

"Rex, you really don't owe me an explanation."

"But I want to give you one, necessary or not. You have to believe me. I haven't thought about another woman since kissing you. Hell, I haven't even thought about another woman since meeting you. Something tells me you might be more than enough for me to handle. I'm not exactly the monogamous type, but I haven't even wanted to explore other options. Whatever we've got going on here, and I'm not sure there's a name for it, is it not something that I was trying to disrespect."

Kit stayed in place and searched for the right words.

"I don't know what this is either." She shrugged. "If anything at all, but I have a lot going on right now, and I certainly do not want you to feel like you have to wait for me to figure all of this out."

"Hey, hey, hey." He tucked a piece of hair behind her ear. "I understand and I do not expect any promises or guarantees. All I know is that I was just filling time before meeting you and waiting until something better came along and, as you can see, it never did. So this is me telling you that I'll wait until this all makes sense. This is as honest as it gets, and we'll will figure it out as it comes. Can we agree on that at least?"

Tears filled her eyes and she nodded slowly.

He grabbed her in a bear hug and kissed the top of her head. "Now, come on, you've had an extremely long day, and I hate to tell you, but you need to shower. You smell like a bonfire."

Kit laughed and some of the tension relieved itself.

The elevators opened and they stepped inside. She leaned on him in a comforting way for support, as if she had done it a thousand times. He rubbed her arm and admired the way she fit against him.

Rex squeezed her gently. "I've never been a patient man, but maybe some things are worth waiting for."

೧⁊೧

They stopped to grab her clothes, but decided to stay at his house for a change of scenery.

"I have got to shower. I can no longer stand myself."

"Please do," he said, smiling.

"Oh, please. You don't smell any better."

"I plan on getting in, but ladies first."

"Such a Southern gentleman. Who knew you had it in you?"

Rex swatted her rear. "Better make it fast or you'll take all the hot water."

Kit started the shower and let the steam fill the room while she undressed. She stared at her reflection the foggy mirror until she could no longer see. She was full of scrapes and bruises that she was just now noticing, and her body ached as she stretched her tired muscles. She began removing the bandage that EMS had applied to her side.

Apparently, she had been cut by a shard of glass while going through the window.

It was sore to the touch as she picked at the sticky tape and her skin looked angry and red beneath it.

"Here let me help you with that," Rex said quietly, concern filling his eyes as he joined her. "I didn't know you got hurt."

"I must have been while I was going through the window. My adrenaline was pumping so much I didn't even feel it, until the medics stopped me. I'm fine, really," she said awkwardly as she became aware she was standing in front of him naked and exposed.

She crossed her arms in front of her in an attempt to cover up while he gently peeled away her bandage.

"I think I have some disinfectant and gauze around here somewhere so we can reapply."

"Thank you," she said, embarrassed.

"Don't do that. Act ashamed of your body in front of me. You're a vision." He touched her arm gently to avoid scaring her away.

"I've not been naked and vulnerable with a man since Andy." Her voice shook as she tried to explain.

"I know," Rex said gruffly. "And I told you I would wait, but I promise when I get to touch you, I will treat you kindly."

He stood shirtless in a pair of worn jeans and his muscles, toned from daily use, made him look all the more desirable.

She bit her lower lip and slowly uncrossed her arms to reveal her body. Goosebumps pricked her skin, despite the warm steam. She opened the shower door and cautiously stepped inside never breaking eye contact.

Rex understood the silent invitation, slowly unbuckled his jeans, and stepped out of them when they slid to the floor. He stepped inside the shower beside her and closed the door. He wanted her before, but he did not want to make any sudden moves that would leave her feeling like he took advantage of her vulnerable situation.

Kit turned to face him and let the hot spray pound over her head. She closed her eyes and let the warm water relax her body. Soot and grime cascaded to the shower floor and watching the water flow down her body trickling across her erect nipples was too much for his manhood not to react.

When she opened her eyes she could not help but notice, and she held a look of innocent surprise.

"Don't worry about me," he said in a low voice. "I have no control over these things. Watching you is like taking ecstasy." He grabbed a bottle of shampoo. "Do you need a hand?"

Without a word, she turned and let him lather up her hair. His fingers massaged her scalp and the soap made her body slick.

He leaned her back to rinse off the bubbles, careful to avoid her eyes. Pouring some soap onto a loofa, he began working it across her body in small circular motions, avoiding the bumps and bruises she had acquired during the fire.

When the soap had reached the cut on her side, she winced when she felt the burn.

He stopped immediately and grabbed her. "Are you okay?"

"I am fine," she said. "I swear."

His eyes flashed with anger. "I ought to kill him for hurting you, and if I get my hands on him, I just might."

"Shhh, Rex." She placed a finger across his lips. "Let's not spoil this moment thinking about him. There are not many times that I'm not thinking about it, and just now in this moment, I wasn't."

Rex kissed the inside of her palm, as his erection hardened. "I promise to protect you."

"I know you do," she whispered. "For now, just let me wash you. It is my turn."

Kit grabbed the soap and lathered the loofa until it was nice and sudsy. She rubbed it across the taut muscles of his shoulder blades and down to his tight rear. She took her time exploring the feel of him and enjoyed getting to know his body.

He sucked in his breath when she made her way to the front.

She hesitated momentarily before touching him there and, even with his eyes closed he sensed her reservation.

"There's no pressure. You do not have to do anything you don't want to," he said hoarsely, trying to remain patient, but his need was growing greater.

"No, I want to," she said quickly. "I do. I just have not had as much practice at this as you have. It is a little intimidating."

She lowered her eyes, and Rex tilted her chin upward. "You, Kit Harwick, have nothing to be intimidated by. You're driving me crazy." He shuddered and laughed softly. "Come here."

Rex leaned down and kissed her passionately. Kit met his lips with willingness and the moment they connected, the chemistry ignited.

The kiss deepened and their hands were all over each other in a mix of slippery wetness and steamy bubbles.

He angled her breast toward his mouth and claimed it eagerly. She watched as his mouth worked over her, and she moaned in delight.

"Rex," she whispered.

He looked up at her. The sound of his name escaping her lips was music to his ears.

He recognized the look in her eyes, stood abruptly, and grabbed her legs while backing her up against the wall of the shower. She wrapped them around his waist as he stared her straight in the eye and waited a moment.

She nodded for him to proceed. "Rex, please."

That was all the confirmation he needed, and he thrust upward as he entered her swiftly.

Her head fell back, both of them breathing heavy. They came together quickly, and her head fell against his shoulder in the ultimate release.

He held her there pinned between his body and the slick wall while he caught his breath. When he lowered her feet back to the ground, he kissed her gently before meeting her eyes again.

"Are you okay?" Compassion filled his voice.

"I'm more than okay," she assured him.

"Good." He affectionately rolled his forehead across hers and interlaced his fingers through hers. "Because, in a few minutes, I'm sure your brain is going to go a million miles a minute trying to scrutinize and examine this from every possible angle. I'm asking you not to. Just relax and enjoy."

She laughed easily. "Actually, Mr. Know it all, I was wondering when we could do that again."

"Be careful what you wish for," he said as he switched off the water and scooped her up into his arms. She squealed as he tossed her on the bed.

CHAPTER 18

They napped in between their lovemaking and whispered into the wee hours of the night, like a couple of school kids.

"So when are we leaving for Watertown?"

"What?" she asked, surprised.

"I heard Mellie say that you were going to a memorial for Andy. Since there is no way I'm letting you go without protection, it looks like I'm going to Watertown too. So when do we leave?"

She placed her hand on his cheek. "I appreciate your understanding. I need to be there for Andy and his memory, but I also want to have a meeting with Sergeant Hunter to get updated on the case. He called to let me know they would be looking into any disgruntled citizens that Andy had dealings with, and the past two messages were sent to the handwriting experts. I'm hoping that they have some leads before we get there."

"Are you going to answer me about when we are supposed to leave?"

"The memorial is November first, and I thought we could get there a day early for the ground work," she said scrunching her nose. "Is that okay?"

"That's the day after…" He looked at his watch. "…the day after today, as in tomorrow?"

"I know it's short notice, so if you can't go I understand."

"No, I can switch some shifts around and make it work."

She smiled sweetly. "Thank you."

"I'm starving. Should we eat now so you can get to the hospital early?"

"Perfect." Kit swung her legs over the side of the bed, searching frantically for her nightclothes.

"Hey." He kissed her hard on the mouth. "You were amazing."

Kit blushed and giggled all the way to the kitchen, where there was a knock on the door.

She glanced out the window before opening the door. "Rex, it's Brady."

"Kit." Brady tipped his hat. "Sorry to disturb you so early, but I wanted to make sure I caught you. Do you mind if I talk to my brother for a moment?"

"What brings you to my house at this time of day? Did something happen?" Rex asked.

"No, no nothing like that. I just wanted to congratulate you on a job well done at the fire yesterday. You were a real hero, and for the first time, I got a real glimpse of what you must have left behind in New York. Their loss was our gain."

Rex eyed Brady suspiciously. "Thanks, I guess. What are you up to Brady?"

"Nothing, man, I don't want to start any trouble. Look, I know there was no love lost between you and our father, and that trickled down between you and me. I'll take my blame for my part of the responsibility. But, man, we were just kids. I'm grown now and know better. I just wanted to let you know that I'm sure it looked like I had it all and, in some ways, I did, and I'm sorry for that, but Dad was not an easy man to get along with, even when he stuck around. He was a hard son of a bitch, and I'm ashamed to admit there were times in my childhood that I was jealous of you not having to deal with him. Stupid, I know, but your momma was a real nice lady, and she did not deserve any of the hard breaks she got. I know that she was really proud of you, and I hope you take comfort in that."

Rex sucked his teeth and looked out in the distance. "You came by this morning to tell me all that?"

"I reckon it has been weighing on my mind for some time now, years even, if we're being honest. I know we've always had a not-so-friendly rivalry, probably created most in part by dear old Dad, but I have never really felt good about it, and it's probably high time we put an end to it.

"We've shared some words recently regarding Kit, and you can't really blame a man for trying. She seems like a real nice girl, just got herself in a bit of a bad way, but she deserves better than all that. I thought I would be a man about it and tell you that you two seem real nice together. I don't know what your intentions are, and it's really none of my business, but it's a pleasure to see you care about something again."

Brady sighed. "So anyhow, you don't have to worry about me getting in your way. My focus is the case and if you two need anything at all, I'm at your service. I would like to work together if at all possible."

Rex rocked back on his heels and spoke slowly. "I think that can be possible."

"Good. I'm done stroking your ego for the day, but I thought you should know all the guys on the scene yesterday were bragging on you. So it was a job well done. Y you should be proud of yourself. Just a show of good faith, I wrote up a letter of commemoration to the chief. I hope it pays off one day." Brady started to walk away and stopped at the stairs. "You know, I always wanted a brother, and I'm sorry our father ruined that for us. He should have been there for you, especially when you needed him the most. I can't speak for him as far as the way of apologies go, but on my behalf, I am sorry."

Rex walked forward and, for a moment, Brady wondered if he was going to push him down the stairs, but he stuck his hand out instead, which almost caught Brady equally off guard.

Brady joined his hand in a firm shake.

"That took guts, man. I'll give you that, and…well, I appreciate it. Who knows? Maybe one day, we can work toward that brother title, but for now though, we can start by being friends."

"I'd like that," Brady said. "Enjoy your breakfast and give Mellie my best. I would tell you to keep an eye on Kit, but I know you already are."

"You got it."

Rex stood there in the early morning sun watching Brady pull away, not realizing how long he had waited for those words.

☙☙☙

"What was all that about?" Kit asked when Rex reentered the kitchen.

She had been standing on her tiptoes over the kitchen sink trying to peer out the window in case a brawl started.

Rex walked over to her and squeezed her around her middle. "I think he came here as a brother to tell me I did a good job yesterday."

"Really?" she asked, raising her eyebrows. "That was nice."

"And to tell me that he thought we looked real nice together, and he's glad to see me happy."

Kit arched back so she could see his face. "Really?" she said again.

"Really. I barely believe it myself. There was something in there about apologizing for the past too."

"Rex, that's amazing. Maybe there's hope for you two yet."

"Maybe. The world's full of surprises, both good and bad."

"It certainly is," she said, hugging him in a tight embrace.

Before she knew it, Rex had stiffened, and she pulled away to see what the problem was.

Tears had pooled in his eyes and, for the first time, he did not have the hard, tough-as-nails look in them that she was accustomed to seeing.

"Oh, Rex, honey, this is a good thing."

"I know," he said, wiping them away fiercely. "I just had not realized how much I needed to hear it."

Kit hugged him tight and let him relieve himself of all his childhood anger.

When he was through she said, "Now, let's go see Mellie to hopefully get some more good news."

₧₧₧

"She looked good, didn't she?" Kit asked him for the third time.

"Yes, she looked good," Rex reassured her.

"I just feel so guilty about leaving. What if something happens?"

"Nothing is going to happen. She's in a great facility with the best care. No one can get to her there, and that woman is so loved, she will not have a shortage of visitors. You heard her tell you to go and take care of business."

"I know, but I feel like this is all my fault that she's in there in the first place."

"Kit, this is not your fault. This is the doings of an obviously mentally unstable person. You heard the fire chief. The man poured gasoline on her house and lit it on fire. He shot a police officer and has been terrorizing you. He's obviously a nut job, and when he's run through the lab data base, there'll be a hit because there's no way this kook has held it together until now."

"And then he'll be caught, and we can move on with our lives," she breathed.

"That's right and until then, you're safe with me."

"I don't know about all that. You can be kind of scary," she teased.

"And it's best that you remember that and keep a man happy."

"Oh, you think so. It's a two way street."

"And I promise to return the favor." He nuzzled her ear as they walked toward his house.

Suddenly, they both noticed they were not alone. Lisa was sitting on the steps. "Rex. Kit."

"What are you doing here?" Rex asked with an edge to his voice.

"I'm sorry to show up unannounced, but it was important that I speak to you both. I don't want any problems. I made a mistake in coming here yesterday, and I realize that now and hope you can forgive me. Would it be all right if I come in? I've got some things to tell you."

"What could you possibly say to us that we would care to hear?" Rex asked, resentment filling his voice, but

Kit grabbed his arm to stop him, noticing the wide-eyed look on Lisa's face.

"Let her finish, Rex. What is it, Lisa? What's wrong?"

Lisa wrung her hands nervously. "I think I've seen the man who's stalking you."

"I think we better go inside." Kit ushered her in to the kitchen.

"I've already been to the police and made a full report. They had me talk to a sketch artist, and I gave them the best description I could. The man said his name was John Adams, but I now know that was a lie. It was always dark, and we were drinking, and I don't know how honest of a representation it was, but I want ya'll to know that I did my best. It was not until I heard people talking about what was going on that I realized he was not who he said he was. I promise if I had known, I would have never talked to him," she said, crying softly.

Kit clutched her hand and Rex was amazed at the amount of empathy she could show toward Lisa.

"You couldn't have known. Tell us everything you do know."

Lisa started from the very first night she had met John. "He said that he was romantically involved with Kit and that she had just up and dropped him and moved away. He used my vulnerability and obvious jealousy to his advantage. He just made it seem like we were connected by being heartbroken over the two of you, and we were both pissed at the amount of time you were spending together. I did find it odd how much effort he wanted to spend spying on you, but I admit that I, too, was curious about what was going on with Rex and the new girl. My pride was damaged at how quickly I was pushed to the wayside as if I never really mattered at all, but that doesn't justify how we invaded your privacy."

"I'm sorry that I hurt you," Rex said honestly. "I was under the impression that we both understood it was a casual thing."

"I did know that. I guess I was just hoping you'd change your mind. I want you to know that I had no idea this man was a psychopath and meant to do you real harm. I didn't have any knowledge of or participate in any way with the notes he left for you or with setting the fire. When I heard all of that, it made my blood run cold. I knew he seemed to drink a lot, but he must really be out of his mind. It makes me sick to know that I was sitting next to a cold-blooded killer."

"You're an extremely lucky girl that he didn't hurt you. Going along with him and his demented scheme was probably the best for your safety," Kit said genuinely. "I would lay low for a while now that you're not on his team, and I appreciate you coming to us with this information. If you can think of anything else at all, please call me. I'll give you my cell number and, Lisa, if he reaches out to you in any way, you go directly to the police. He's a very dangerous man. You need to be extremely careful."

"I will, thank ya'll for your kindness and understanding. I hope they catch him soon."

"Me too," Kit said.

"Take care, Lisa. Will you be okay getting home?" Rex asked.

"I'll be all right. The police are providing extra patrols and things like that. Besides, it's not me he's after." She paused. "He's entirely consumed by Kit.'

Kit tried not to react, but chills ran up and down her spine.

CHAPTER 19

Brady brought the sketch by Rex's house while he and Kit packed. When she saw the picture, it struck a chord in her. There was something familiar about him, but she could not put her finger on it. She felt like she had seen him before, but where? It nagged at her until she had a headache. She rubbed her temples and sighed in frustration.

"You can't force it, Kit. It will come to you when you least expect it. Brady, do you think we could keep this copy in case something sparks in her memory?"

"Of course, and I already faxed a copy over to Watertown PD. Sergeant Hunter was going to ask around to see if anybody recognizes our suspect."

"Thank you, Brady."

"Now you two have a safe trip. Hopefully 'John Adams' is caught and behind bars by the time you get back."

"He won't be staying in Middle Bay," Kit said.

"What do you mean?"

"He's too narcissistic for that. He'll want to be at that memorial for Andy, to take credit for what he's done. If it's me he wants, he'll follow me wherever I go.

He won't let me out of his sight for a couple days. His focus this entire time has been on forcing me to remember the anniversary of Andy's death, to make me relive what happened a year ago, so there is no way he won't be there for the actual date. He has gotten more reckless and menacing in his actions. He wants me to notice him. He wants me to be afraid. He wants to take everything I know and love away from me, and then he wants me gone, and I think he is getting tired of waiting. And so far, his plan is working."

✑✑✑

That night Kit lay awake, listening to Rex's soft snore and the mating calls of the tree frogs. She could not decide if it was borderline beautiful or if the repetitiveness was annoying. In any event, it was not the noise that was keeping her awake. It was the thought that this stalker could be anywhere, anytime, and she felt like he was closing in. The sketch of his face was imprinted in her mind, and she saw it everywhere, especially when she closed her eyes. Shadows loomed everywhere, and the dark corners now appeared even more ominous, obscure, and threatening.

She felt a general feeling of fear and impending doom. This was not going to end amicably and without altercation, and she could feel her anxiety growing.

Their bags were packed, and, tomorrow, they were leaving to go back to Watertown, the place where this all started and maybe where it would inevitably end. One way or the other.

Sometime in the night, her eyes fell shut, and she let herself drift off to sleep. Her body grew heavy as she let go of her consciousness one limb at a time.

Suddenly, a blast sounded, and glass sprayed across the bed, causing her to shoot upright immediately. It took her eyes a moment to focus before she realized something had flown through the window next to where she was sleeping.

She reached out to shake Rex, but he was already jumping out of bed and pulling on his jeans.

"Rex, he's here. Be careful there is glass everywhere."

"Are you okay?" he asked.

"I think so," she replied, but when she moved, she was being pricked by a million shards of glass.

"Come here, grab my neck."

She did as she was told, and he scooped her up out of the mess, setting her bare feet down where the floor was clear of debris.

"Wait here," he said and reached under the bed for his loaded shot gun.

"Please, Rex. Don't go out there. I'm begging you. I just have a really bad feeling." She pulled on his arm. "Stay here with me."

"Kit, I promise I'll be back."

She began sobbing hysterically as he marched onto the porch.

"Come on out, you no good coward. You're a real tough guy when you're hiding behind your veiled threats and preposterous puzzle pieces. Come on out, and we will handle this man to man. We will see how tough you really are."

Kit closed her eyes and began praying with all her might. She felt paralyzed with terror as she sat hugging her knees. She had no idea how long she stayed like that, but it was long enough her muscles began to ache from being frozen with fear.

When she heard heavy booted footsteps approaching,

she squeezed her eyes shut even tighter, and her breaths came in short and choppy, on the verge of hyperventilation.

"Come here, baby. You're all right. It's just me," Rex whispered in her ear. He rocked her back and forth in his arms until her muscles released, and she wept in his arms.

"It's too much. It's all just too much."

"I know. I know," he said, rubbing her hair. "I've got you."

When she opened her eyes, she let out a shaky breath and looked over at the window. "I wonder what he threw."

She carefully stepped over glass to investigate. Half hidden under the bed was a cement brick. She picked it up and turned it over.

On it, it said:

I'll see you in Watertown.

Taped beside the message was the corner piece of the puzzle, leaving only the middle piece empty. She gasped and handed it to Rex.

"It looks like your suspicions were right," he said grimly. "Come on, let's go."

"Where are we going, the police?" she asked, following him.

"Nope, rise and shine, sweetheart. It doesn't look like we're going to get anymore sleep. We're headed to Watertown."

ⅇⱱⅇⱱ

From his hiding spot in the woods, he saw them turn their headlights on and pull away. He had gotten a kick out of the way Rex had tried to act like Rambo—holding his gun yelling out obscenities—knowing that he could see Rex, but Rex could not see him.

He had wanted Kit to know how close he could get to her without her knowing. He wanted her to be nervous at all times, never knowing when he would strike. The game was coming to an end and, although he looked forward to the grand finale, he would feel some sadness when it was all over.

He enjoyed watching her squirm and as more people got involved, it became more of a challenge to hide out. He had to work harder at covering his tracks and the police had come close to him a couple of times as they shined their lights near his location.

He knew he had to be careful. That was why he mostly worked at night. The dark country roads made it nearly impossible to see. He had given up finding a place to sleep and had mostly crashed in his truck or camped out near it. Pickup trucks were a dime a dozen in good ol' Arkansas, but he had made sure to change the plates periodically.

He never ventured into town when anyone would notice, and since there was a rest stop just on the outskirts, he was able to clean up in the sink, although even to him, he was getting pretty ripe and knew he needed a real shower.

He carried various IDs that he had made in advance and the liquor store that sold him his adult beverages also housed homemade pornos which attracted some pretty seedy characters. He was surrounded by some Baptist-loving dry counties so it was not odd that this type of establishment brought out the sinners and cheats. Compared to the rest of them, he blended in perfectly fine. With a little facial hair, he was barely recognizable and with all the truckers passing through, locals did not even think to look at him twice.

He waited to get good and drunk until he was by himself. He had had at least that much sense, and his diligence had paid off because he had nearly completed all of his tasks.

Admittedly it would have been easier had she not found a male companion, but it proved he was even better at his covert operations than he had given himself credit for.

Overall, he was feeling pretty proud of himself as he took another swig of his whiskey. It did not bother him a bit that they would beat him to Watertown as he expected that was where they were headed. With the GPS tracker he had installed on Rex's truck, he would know where they were at all times.

Rex did not even now when he had attached the device. He had been too preoccupied taking care of poor Kit and her fragile mental state, and making sweet love to her, to notice.

He was prepared. He knew Watertown like the back of his hand. He had spent over a year making sure he was prepared, and it all led up to this.

He had one shot, and he planned to make it count. He would like to get Kit up close and personal in her final moments, but if that just was not possible, he had his faithful stolen high-profile rifle, with a scope so accurate that he surely would not miss. It was times like this he was thankful that Daddy had made him hunt. He just did not know it would be human prey that was caught between his cross hairs. It was amazing what revenge could make a man do.

He never considered himself an animal, but it was a dog-eat-dog world and only the strong survived. He was going to make sure that justice was served. Some people just insisted on learning the hard way, and Kit Harwick was one of them.

∽∾∽

After Rex had called Brady to update him about the ambush that had taken place, they made a pit stop for coffee and to use the restroom.

"If I forget to tell you later, I'm really grateful that you're making this trip with me. I'll pay for the window."

Rex looked over at Kit in the passenger seat. "Forget about the window. It will be fixed before I get back. I'm just glad you're okay. I'm over this sneaky son of a bitch, and I'm going to make him pay."

Kit fell silent.

"Kit, I know this is going to be an emotional trip for you. It's sure to take you down memory lane, and I know it's going to hurt, but I hope at the end of all this, it provides you with a sense of closure so that you can begin to move on with your life, however you decide. I do not plan on getting in the way of that, but I'm here for you in any way that you need me to be."

"Look at you, you started out as a bartender, most eligible bachelor, player, and turns out you are a firefighter, bodyguard, locksmith, painter, lifesaver, lover, brother, and a really good friend. Who knew there were so many great attributes under the harsh exterior of the snarky, cocky, calloused man I once thought you were? You're such a surprise to me."

"I think there was a compliment in there somewhere."

"There was, trust me."

"For what it's worth, I think you're talented, kind, yet sarcastically witty, hard headed, but persevering, warm, innocently charming, and last, but not least, a warrior."

"A warrior? I could not feel further from it."

"Well, it's true. Not many people have cold parents and come out warm, not many people go through what you have and still choose to see the best in people and still have the ability to laugh. There may be darkness all around you when you're looking for the light, but you're the light. I may not be that holy of a man, but, Kit, God put the light in you so that you could shine during the storm."

Kit looked at him in surprise with tears in her eyes.

"What's wrong?"

"Nothing, and everything all at the same time. I don't think anyone has ever said anything that nice to me before."

"Someone should be that nice to you every day, Kit. Do not settle for less than that."

eↄeↄ

Jacob Hunter sat at the computer, scrolling through pages of evidence, most of which he had seen a thousand times over, but he hoped, more than anything, today something would stand out. He had received the fax of the sketch of their suspect and, unfortunately, it could match a number of law-abiding, hunting, beer-drinking citizens in this very town.

Nevertheless, he attempted to compare it to previous mugshots of the regulars they had dealt with before. He wanted to solve this case, but not just because it was any case. This would answer who killed Slade.

He had been there that night. One of his best friends was shot. He was two feet away when he watched him slump to the ground. Jay had done everything his training had told him to do.

He covered the bullet hole with his own hands and done CPR when Andy quit breathing. He pleaded with him to hang on as he helped load him into the ambulance.

He had waited in the hospital waiting room while Slade was in surgery and held Kit up when they delivered the news that he did not make it.

That night had haunted him ever since, plaguing him during the day and revisiting him in his nightmares. It was personal.

This man was beyond another criminal. He was a cop killer, and not just any cop killer, but was guilty of killing one of Jay's own. Now he was terrorizing Kit, who Jay thought of as family.

The killer had walked free for almost a year, but Jay was determined to put an end to him by any means necessary. You did not mess with family, and Jay would go to the grave knowing he did everything he could to make this bastard pay.

He knew he was missing something, something vital that would show him the way. This was not a random act, but premeditated so he needed to get inside of the man's mind.

What would make him go to the length of hatred that this man did? Only if someone hurt his family, his wife, and kids, could he see performing such acts.

If someone did something to his family. The thought stuck with him. One of the messages sent to Kit said an *Eye for an eye. He took away my family, and now I take away yours.* Jay knew he had to narrow down his search to someone who had his family taken away. Someone who had a bad taste in their mouth toward cops, Slade in particular. Someone with knowledge of guns and who liked to drink in large amounts. Someone focused on the year anniversary of Andy's death, and most importantly, someone who had nothing to lose.

CHAPTER 20

W hen they arrived, a brick wall holding a plague announced they had entered Watertown.

Kit clutched the door handle as anticipation filled her. "This is it. We're here."

"Where are we headed?" Rex asked.

"We'll need to check into the only hotel in town, The Sunset, but first do you mind taking me past my old house? I know it hasn't been long, but I'd like to see it."

"Of course. Just give me the directions."

Kit navigated him to the south end of town to a small subdivision where her house was the lone ranger on a culd-a-sac.

"That's it there."

Rex drove slowly, whistling at where she had come from.

"It is smaller on the inside than what it looks like on the outside," she explained. "But it was home." She kept her face toward the glass as memories poured over her. "The new owners took down the bushes, but it's basically the same. They added a tire swing for their son I see. I bet he likes that. This was a great place to raise kids," she said wistfully.

"Do you want to get out and go look?"

"No," she said reluctantly. "It is no longer mine. After Andy, it felt too vacant. It was not a place to live by yourself. I tried to keep up with it, but it eventually just became too much and was a constant reminder. This place deserved a family and hustle and bustle, crumbs on the floor, and basketballs hitting the garage door, not the solitude and tear-stained pillows that I provided it."

He squeezed her hand. "Okay, where to next?"

"There's a little place called the Water Tree Café. We can go there for a late breakfast before we check in."

"That sounds good. I'm starving and could use a cup of Joe."

"Great, first, do you mind if we stop by the police station."

He looked at her seriously. "The scene of the crime?"

"I can't wait forever, and I need to see it."

ↄ৽ↄ

Rex pulled into the police department parking lot and turned off the engine. Kit sat for a moment, looking at the building silently, and Rex left her to her thoughts. She took a deep breath and wiped her clammy hands on her pants legs.

With trepidation, she slowly pulled the door handle open and slid out of the truck.

He waited a moment, while she walked the premise slowly, before getting out to follow her.

She pulled down her sunglasses and wiped a lone tear from her face. "They think the shooter was stationed somewhere by the water tower before entering the building from this direction. Forensics determined he used a high-powered rifle and dropped Andy with one clean shot. By the time they had realized what happened and rushed to Andy's aid, the shooter had returned to his vehicle and had taken off."

Rex squeezed her shoulders from behind.

"They tried to save him, but it was probably doomed from the beginning. The bullet entered his chest and ricocheted off of some internal organs before blowing out his back. The damage had been too much to repair. Sergeant Hunter, who you will meet, was standing mere feet away from where Andy was hit, and he acted fast, but Andy died shortly after at the hospital on his way into surgery. I know that it was hard on Sergeant Hunter, as it has been for everyone."

"I cannot imagine," Rex murmured.

"If anyone can get to the bottom of this, he can, because he is personally invested," Kit said.

"Do you want to go in?"

"I suppose I should."

"Whenever you are ready." He held her hand in a show of support.

"Might as well be sooner rather than later," she said and pulled open the front door.

The familiarity hit her as she stepped inside and a moment of nostalgia washed over her when the secretary buzzed them in.

"Well, look who it is," Sherri exclaimed, jumping up from her desk. "I'm so happy to see you. How is the South treating you?"

Kit contemplated everything she had been through the past few weeks and decided it was better not to get into it. "Good, I have settled in nicely."

Sherri eyed Rex and nodded her approval. "I would say indeed it has."

"Sherri, this is Rex Jennings, my neighbor. He was

kind enough to drive me back so I did not have to make the trip alone."

"A Southern gentlemen. Do you have a friend for me?"

Kit snorted. "I do not know about all that."

Rex laughed. "Kit's right, but it's nice to meet you mam."

"Oh, an accent. I love me some accents. Are there real cowboys where you come from?"

"Well, we have cows and men that take care of them that act more like boys if that is what you mean."

Sherri let out a belly laugh. "And a sense of humor, a real charmer."

"Okay, we've got to get out of here before his head explodes. Is Jay around by chance?"

"Oh, you're lucky you came when you did. Most of the guys just went to lunch, but he has been locked away in his office working away on something. I'll call him up. He'll be so happy to see you."

"Thanks, Sherri, it was good to see you."

"You too, sweetheart, do not be such a stranger now."

"I won't," Kit said with a promise that she was not sure she would keep.

&&&

Jay came to the front to meet them and straightened his wrinkled uniform. When she saw him, emotions came flooding back, and she dove into his embrace. They stood hugging for a long time. No words were necessary.

Rex shifted uncomfortably and she suddenly remembered that he was there.

She stepped out of Jay's arms and indicated Rex.

"Jay, this is Rex Jennings. Rex, this is Sergeant Jacob Hunter."

The two men shook hands and Jay said, "Kit said you would be coming with her. That's kind of you to take care of her."

"Thank you, sir. I intend to keep an eye out for her."

"That's good, that's real good," Jay said thoughtfully. "And call me Jay. We don't do formalities around here. You guys are earlier than I expected. You must have made good time."

"Well, we left earlier than expected after an incident."

"Incident? What incident are we talking about?"

"Well, our psychopath struck again. Do you want to go someplace to talk about it? We're starving. I thought I'd take Rex to the cafe."

"Sure, I could use a bite. I've been pouring over evidence and barely consumed enough to sustain myself."

"It's settled then."

"All right, I'll follow you there."

⚭⚭⚭

When they were seated around the small table with red and white checkered tablecloth, Rex excused himself and went to the restroom.

Jay did not waste time getting straight to the point. "So what's the story with Mr. Jennings? Does he treat you right?"

Kit flushed. "It's not like that, he's just a friend. He lives across the lake from me and has been there to help me during some of the difficult circumstances.

"There's no judgment from me, Kit. It was just a question, Andy would want you to be happy, but he would also want me to look out for you. Just doing my duty as Andy's friend."

"And I appreciate that, I really do, but Rex is a good man just helping a girl out. He saved my grandmother's life during the fire, and he used to be a firefighter in New York before his mother got sick and passed."

"Oh, I'm sorry to hear that. He would be a fool not to think more of you, Kit, and I'm glad he's there for you. Just keep your standards high, you hear?"

"Yeah, I hear you."

Rex returned to the table, and without a question, knew they had been talking about him. It did not bother him. He expected nothing less. He just wished he could have been a fly on the wall to hear what Kit had said.

"Okay, so let's get down to business. What happened last night?"

Kit filled him in on the brick being thrown through the window and the message that had been left. She could visibly see Jay tense with anger, and he nearly bent the fork in his hand.

"I'd like to say I'm shocked, but I figured he would make his way back for the memorial. In fact, I almost welcome him to come back on my turf because, this time, we're going to get him. I have been scouring through the evidence both old and new, and I've come to the conclusion that the dates he has chosen are very much on purpose. If that's the case, he plans to attack again on the date of Andy's death."

"I've thought the very same thing," Kit replied. "And you can say it. We all know he plans to attack me."

Jay sat with a grim look on his face that said he could not deny it.

"I thought that, by moving away from the scene of the crime, I could start to put it behind me and make a fresh start, but I realize now how naive I was to think that. This was obviously a well-thought out plan, and he's not about to give up before it's all over. Once I moved, it was one incident after another, almost as if he was becoming more—"

"Desperate to finish what he started," Jay finished for her.

"Exactly."

"I believe that's because of the approaching dates. I've started to look into some of our repeat offenders of people that had a revolving negative track record with the police, Andy in particular. I'm going on a hunch and saying if he is interested in an eye for an eye and he has gone after, first, Andy, and now you and yours, that he has somehow lost his family. What else would provoke someone to have so much hatred?"

Rex spoke up for the first time. "I can see that theory holding up. Someone messes with my family or someone close to me, it could motivate me to do things I would not normally do. What about the sketch? Do you recognize it as someone you have dealt with?"

"It could resemble quite a few people around this town, but I've compared it to some mug shots, which is a slow moving process."

"We'd be happy to help if it would lighten your work load at all," Rex offered.

"I might have to take you up on that. Something else to consider is if he has altered his appearance at all. Coloring or growing out his hair, adding facial hair, etc."

"Well, I also have these," Kit said reaching into her purse and pulling out the puzzle pieces. She laid them out neatly, matching the jigsaw up correctly. "I know it's only the border of the picture, and we're missing the main piece, their faces, but it is obvious that it is a family photo. I've studied these pieces extensively, and the man has a flash of brown hair showing on the top left corner. The right corner shows a glimpse of longer brunette hair and the bottom shows little legs, maybe the bottom of a back-pack. If you look here, it looks like you can see a sippy cup. Mickey Mouse maybe? I only received this piece last night, and I can only assume this is a family photo. What do you think?"

Jay studied the images placed before him closely. "I see it." He tried to study the background, what little he could see. "The trees are mature, not what you would see in a newer subdivision. There's a small shot of the house. It has dirty white siding, it looks like. This might get us somewhere, narrow down our search a bit."

"That's what I was hoping." She bit her lip. "I know he's saving the biggest piece of the puzzle for last, and as much as I want the answers, I do not want to know what it's going to take to get it."

"Kit, I hope we have the answers before it gets to that point. The memorial is tomorrow night and I know our guy will be there. We will make sure you're protect-ed."

"She'll be protected," Rex said in a serious tone.

Jay eyed him, sizing him up. "I appreciate that, as I am sure that Kit does as well, and I know that Andy would say the same. Take care of our girl. We'll have backup at your disposal. I need to get back to it. Unfortu-nately, this is not going to get figured out over pancakes and biscuits and gravy."

"No, I guess not," Kit said, getting out her wallet.

"My treat. It is the least I can do until I can get this guy behind bars."

"Thank you, Jay. I'm going to use the ladies room."

Kit excused herself, leaving the two men alone.

When she was out of ear shot, Jay said, "Look, I'm no Einstein, but I know you're not just friends, and Kit would never admit it out of respect for Andy, but all

Andy or any of us would want for her is to be happy. Just see to it that she is."

Rex eyed the other man seriously. "I'll do my best."

"Good, because believe me when I say, that girl deserves it. She has been through hell and back."

"Understood," Rex replied.

Jay stuck his hand out, and the two men shook on it.

When Kit came back they walked out front.

"Kit, I know words don't mean anything or make the pain go away, but I'm sorry for all that you've been through. Hell, this latest mess, the loss of Andy, and the loss of your baby. I'm so sorry.

"Thanks, Jay," she said wearily. "Call me with any news, okay?"

When they walked back the truck Kit was quiet.

Rex broke the silence. "Baby? What baby?"

Kit sighed. "You caught that, huh?"

CHAPTER 21

After they checked into their room, they dropped their bags, exhausted.

"What baby?" Rex asked her again.

Kit covered her face and then ran her fingers through her hair. "You aren't going to let it go, are you?"

"Not likely," he said. "Kit, talk to me. What was Hunter talking about?"

She took a deep breath and stood. Going to stand by the window, she looked out but was not seeing the view, which was of the parking lot and the meager amount of cars that had guest parking stickers. She was trying to find the words to answer Rex who was waiting anxiously with his hands on his hips.

"A little over a year ago, I found out I was pregnant. I had not been feeling well and although I was taking birth control, I had been prescribed antibiotics for an inner ear infection." She glanced at him and he looked at her as if she had lost him. "Antibiotics can make birth control pills ineffective."

"Oh, I didn''t know that," he said lamely.

"Well, with your track record, that's good information to know."

He rolled his eyes and motioned for her to continue.

"We were aware of the risks, but obviously we threw caution to the wind, believing the chance of that happening was minimal. At first, I thought the medications or the infection itself was making me ill, but when it persisted, I thought I better take a test. To say that I was shocked was an understatement. You see, I have a minor case of polycystic ovarian syndrome. It causes my cycles to be erratic, so I was under the assumption it might be somewhat difficult for me to get pregnant, but I took the pill to help regulate my cycle, not to mention help relieve some horrible cramps." She realized she was rambling. "Anyway, when I saw the two pink lines, I didn't know whether to laugh or to cry. We were about to start planning our wedding, and I never imagined being a pregnant bride, but on the other hand, I believe in fate and felt very blessed that I didn't have the stress of having to try month after month, being disappointed or having to resort to fertility treatment. I wanted to get it confirmed by a doctor before telling Andy. I guess it just seemed a little too good to be true. So I went in and had blood work done, and the doctor's office called me the next day. The nurse clarified, saying, 'You are definitely pregnant, and your levels suggest we are at a point we can do an ultrasound.'

"I got in the very next day. I guess they could sense my nervousness and reservations to be happy. Low and behold, there was a little baby in there, and even more thrilling was seeing it's tiny fluttering heartbeat. The tech asked if I wanted to hear it. I thought that was a silly question. It was music to my ears. I took a video of it so that I could show Andy. When he came home after a long shift, he asked if I wanted a glass of wine. I said, although that sounded fabulous, I wanted to show him something first. I got out the video and played it. He looked confused at first and then in awe. He said, 'Is that what I think it is?' I answered, 'It is your baby's heartbeat, Daddy.' I'll never forget the look on his face. Shock mixed with a tiny bit of fear, but mostly excitement and pure joy.

"We agreed not to tell anyone until we were further along and knew what we planned to do about the wedding, but Andy couldn't help himself and immediately told some of his coworkers. I wasn't mad, I was happy to see his excitement. We scheduled a follow up appointment. Due to me being on birth control when we conceived, we just wanted to make sure that everything was continuing as it should be. The tears flowed from his eyes freely as we saw our growing bean and an even stronger heart rate. Our little one was even already moving around, although I couldn't feel it yet. I felt like the luckiest person on the planet that I could be a mom and Andy was the father. Although it was early, we started making plans, plans for a nursery and vetoing each other's name choices. We decided on a unisex name of Finlay Cooper Slade. Everything was perfect, until the night of November seventh. My entire world was ripped out from underneath me and all my plans went to hell. I was going to be a single mother. My child would never know their dad. I don't know how many people told me to try to stay calm, that stress was not good for the baby.

"Obviously, I wanted to be the best I could be for my child, but how could I not stress? I'd just lost the love of my life. We were supposed to be a team. As sad as I was, I was happy to be carrying on a piece of Andy's memory inside of me. It was as if by doing that I kept a part of him alive.

"The day of Andy's funeral, I started spotting and, although doctors told me that could be normal, I, of course, was panicked. When they checked me out, the baby was still there, but no longer had a heartbeat. It was the second worst day of my life. They measured the fetus and determined that the baby had quit growing a couple of days prior. It measured almost exactly to the day Andy died.

"They gave me the option of taking meds to help me pass the tissue naturally, as they put it, but that could take weeks, or a D and C surgery where they would remove the baby immediately. The thought of carrying our dead baby around in my womb, not knowing when the act of passing would happen was just too much to bear. So I opted for surgery. I had the small amount of remains cremated and mixed with Andy's ashes.

"The only comfort I had was that he had taken the baby with him, and they're together now. Truth be told, on some of my darkest nights, anger would creep in, and I felt like Andy selfishly took the baby for himself. I know that makes me sound awful, but I was angry for him leaving me here. Why couldn't he have a different job, why did he have to work all the overtime, why couldn't I at least keep my baby, and why was I left there alone to hurt this way? I've come to terms with my feelings toward him. It was just part of my grief, but I still feel hatred toward the man who caused so much heartache, and I worry that my heart is going to stay hard.

"So now you know everything, Rex. It isn't a pretty story, and I'm not an easy woman. I'm broken, no matter how hard I try to fix it. Now excuse me. I'm exhausted and need a shower."

She started to walk away, but he grabbed her arm turning her to face him.

Tears shone in her eyes.

"Kit, I'm so very sorry about everything you've had to go through. All of it. A lesser person would be broken and rightfully so, but your heart could never be hard. It's too big and you're too kind for that. You're one of the most genuine, caring, sweetest people I've ever met. Beautiful on the inside as well as on the outside. Don't count yourself short. There's too much good in you for anyone to take that away."

Tears spilled down her cheeks. "How do you know that? You barely know me."

"It doesn't take long to see that you shine brighter than the rest."

She bit her lip as he wiped away her tears.

"And I'm deeply sorry about your baby. He or she has a beautiful mother they're looking down on. They're excited to meet her one day. One day, long from now, you'll be reunited."

Kit's sob caught in her throat and Rex pulled her close to let her cry it out.

જાજી

Rex watched her as she slept. She had finally cried herself to sleep. She was right. He had not known her long, but what did time have to do with anything? All this taught him was that time was not guaranteed to anyone and shouldn't be taken for granted.

After his mother passed, he was afraid to open himself up to anyone, for fear of experiencing loss or hurting again, but he realized now that he had been wrong, that was no way to live and the opposite was true. You should hold your loved ones even closer and cherish the precious time you had together. His mother had raised him on her own, not something that was planned and certainly not an easy task, but she had always made him feel loved and never a burden. She was proud to be his mom and never had a bitter bone in her body, even until her dying day.

Kit had been raised by two cold and selfish people, not even staying by their daughter's side through the loss of their grandchild or to help her grieve the loss of her fiancé. Yet, she was compassionate and loving.

If these two strong women could find it within themselves to overcome the odds, hell, so could he. Kit had opened his eyes to the future rather than wallowing in the past. He could never repay her for that, but he would not leave her side. He would focus on letting go of his own anger.

Just as soon as this cold-blooded bastard was caught. He was angry for Kit and what she had been through. Just watching her sleep like an angel, he felt an overwhelming sense of peace he had longed for, and come hell or high water, he was not going to let anyone take that away.

ⅇⅎⅇⅎ

After sleeping off the drink from the night before, he had finally made it back to Watertown. He would have to be more careful here as he would be more easily recognizable. He was growing more and more anxious as the time for completing his plan drew nearer.

Knowing that he had scared Kit and angered Rex made his heart soar and race with anticipation. He wanted them to feel the uncertainty and doom that his family had had to face.

The time was getting closer, he could feel the clock ticking, and he was enjoying the feeling of having purpose again. This was not the way he saw his life going, not at all, but he would be damned if he sat by idly while his children had been taken away from him. His wife had been through enough, and he knew he partly had himself to blame, but didn't she know she had vowed for better or worse? Where was her loyalty? She just thought she had to take the police's advice and up and move away with the only things that ever mattered to him?

It was not fair, and someone had to pay the consequences. So he slipped the note under the door of their hotel room and walked away, feeling proud of himself.

They were all in for a rude awakening. Gone were the days the police made the rules, and gone were the days they held all the power.

It was his time now. Time he took back control over his life and what was rightfully his. It was time they were awakened. Their actions had consequences, and it was time they paid the price.

Tomorrow, they would know who they were dealing with and their questions would be answered. They should be scared, very scared indeed.

಼ಲ಼

Kit woke up groggy, and her eyes were grainy from dehydration and all her crying. She had purged her emotions until there was nothing left.

Rex had finally fallen asleep, and she did not want to disturb him so she quietly escaped from out beneath the covers to retreat to a much-deserved shower.

She let the water run hot on full blast, scalding her skin. She needed to feel clean after traveling, crying, and fear had seeped from her pores. She lathered her entire body twice before feeling like she had washed away the grit and she was rejuvenated again.

She stepped out into the small foggy room and toweled herself off before applying lotion to her warm damp skin. She wrapped one towel around her body and one around her wet hair, self-consciously not wanting to walk out undressed, although Rex had already seen her in the most vulnerable state.

When she walked out of the bathroom, she noticed a white envelope underneath the door. Her heart hammered inside of her chest, and she reached for it, wondering how long ago it had been left.

It was a small piece of paper that read:

Glad to see you are back in Watertown. Now the fun begins. I will be seeing you soon.

"Rex," she screamed. "Wake up."

Rex rolled over quickly. "What is it? What's the matter?"

"He's been here. He knows where we are."

CHAPTER 22

The morning was gloomy, the sky was gray, and Kit barely slept a wink throughout the night. After delivering the card to Jay, she and Rex had gotten some carry-out burgers and lay low to avoid another scare.

She dreaded this day and now it was here, she did not want to open her eyes for fear that she would actually have to face it. A year ago on this day, she had been at home writing her book, a mystery, romance that she had hoped would be a best seller. She had dreams and aspirations to be a writer. Although she loved teaching, that was not what she saw as her forever job.

Andy had supported the time and effort she had put in to her writing, and after finding out she was pregnant, she had pushed herself to finish it, knowing with a new baby, time would be limited, and she could not afford to quit her job without another income. All of that fell by the wayside after the loss of Andy and the baby. She had lost her spark. She put her hours in at the daycare and managed to do all that she was supposed to in order to survive, but she would barely call it living, certainly not something Andy would have wanted for her.

She vowed that if she could get through this day, that would all change. Kit needed to get back to the world of the living. The rain matched her mood—a slow drizzle, just enough to be annoying and ruin her hair, but she would live for the sunshine and all the good people and things she had in her life.

Rex rolled over and she was reminded of the man who shared her bed. They had made love just that one time and, out of respect for the circumstances, he had not attempted to since. Rex had made her feel alive, even in the haze of so much tragedy. She did not know when she had come to respect him. Maybe it was the way he handled the fire or maybe even before that when he had taken the time to check on her, but whenever the moment happened, she realized she did respect him, even though at one point she had told him she didn't.

He could have walked away then, escaped the headache, but he did not, and he had quickly become someone she relied on and could depend on. She did not take that lightly.

She needed to get through today and capture Andy's killer, and then she would sort through all of her emotions. She thought Rex was calloused, damaged, and condescending at first, but he turned out to be loving, caring, dependable, and kind. He surprised her even if he did have a rough exterior. Everyone had a past and their own story, and he was just trying to overcome his as was she.

Kit lay there, thinking this could be some story. One day, when she had the heart to put it on paper. She just had to choose to live in order to do it. Suddenly, she wanted nothing more than the simple joys of losing herself, putting words down in print. It was therapeutic and something she longed to feel again.

It reminded her of another day when she had been

writing for hours, and Andy had interrupted her in hopes of romance. His radio went off cutting their time short when he was called in early for a domestic disturbance. She had been disappointed, aggravated, annoyed even, as Andy had said it was a regular he had to deal with. It was the same memory she had dreamt about at the cabin on the lake, the first night Rex had stayed with her.

Wait, that was it. Something about the memory clung on the edge of her mind, telling her that it was not something she should shake away.

Her body went rigid as she tried to remember the exact date of the occurrence. It had been the fall, and it was a Saturday as she was not at work. It was after Halloween because she was eating leftover candy. Could it have been two years ago to this day already?

Rex must have sensed her distress because he rolled over lazily to drape an arm across her. "You awake, teach? You were awfully restless last night. I could not fall asleep until the storm started this morning. I love sleeping in stormy weather, don't you? It's the best kind of weather for cuddling."

"Rex, stop," she screeched.

His eyes popped open, and he sat upright. "What is it? What's wrong?"

"I think I might have remembered something very important that could lead us straight to the killer. In fact, I have been dreaming about it off and on for some time. I think that Andy has been trying to tell me who is behind this the whole time." She was out of bed in a flash. "I have got to tell Hunter."

"Okay, just wait a second. I will throw some clothes on."

"Okay, but I get better cell reception at the end of the hall. I am going to call Jay now. Meet me out there and hurry."

಑಑಑

Kit grabbed her jacket and her phone, shoving her feet into some rain boots before letting herself out of the room. She dialed the numbers, memorized by heart, and held the phone up, going to stand by the window.

"This is Hunter, what's up, Kit?"

"Jay, I think I might have remembered something that is a good lead to who we're looking for. Two years ago, Andy was called into work for a domestic disturbance around this date. I don't know who the subject was, but I know he was annoyed that it was a regular. You might want to look into what case he dealt with. Something tells me it's important."

"Kit, slow down, you're breaking up. Can you hear me?"

Frustrated she looked at her phone to check for service. "Two years ago, Jay. Look in to two years ago," she reiterated. "Can you hear me?"

"What about two years? You're breaking up."

"Stupid phone," she muttered.

She saw an exit door that lead to the stairwell. "Hold on, I am going to move for better service."

She opened the door and a nightmare stared back at her.

"You miss me?" The eerie face smiled behind his unruly beard.

She started to scream.

"Kit are you there?" Hunter asked.

She turned to run, and he clamped a dirty hand over her mouth, while ripping the cell phone out of her other hand and ending the call.

"You are smarter than I gave you credit for," the voice sneered.

She started to fight, but her body weight was no match for his.

"I would not try to resist me," he breathed into her ear.

Ignoring his commands, she began to kick and scratch, bucking beneath his grasp as he tried to drag her down the stairs.

"You like to do things the hard way. Well, two can play at that game," he said before slamming her face against the wall.

Pain seared through her head and then it was if somebody turned the lights out as everything went black.

"That's more like it. I like my women more refined and subdued." He snickered as he dragged her body down the steps and toward the emergency exit where his truck was waiting.

ᗍᘓᗍᘓ

Rex came out of the hotel room carrying a jacket.

"Kit, I could not find an umbrella, but I did bring your toothbrush. I thought you might want to—Kit, where did you go?" He looked around wildly and saw no sign of the woman he swore to protect.

CHAPTER 23

Kit awoke to a throbbing pain that radiated throughout her entire face. The pounding was severe enough that, the minute she regained consciousness, she was instantly nauseated. She became aware that they were driving somewhere. She could feel the vibrations of the tires moving. She kept her eyes closed to avoid her captor knowing she was awake. She felt like he would be less likely to mess with her if she posed no threat to him.

Kit attempted to pay attention to detail by using her other senses. Given an opportunity to reach out for help, she needed to know how to tell them to find her.

The tires were moving quickly over smooth pavement, a highway, she guessed. They were headed out of town because stop lights were fewer and farther between. She listened carefully to sounds around her and believed she heard him spit in a spittoon. *Okay, he chews tobacco.* She made mental notes to herself.

She heard the turning of knobs and the changing of radio stations. Most of them he tried were full of static, but he settled on Tammy Wynette's song, "Stand by your Man."

Kit had liked the song before, but she would never think of it the same from here on out.

He hummed along off key, stopping to hack occasionally. The cab of the truck was enough on its own to make her stomach churn. It reeked of male body odor and stale cigarette smoke. Underneath her feet, bottles rolled around, presumably fifths of whiskey, if she had to guess.

The pungent smell of cheap bourbon had been overwhelming powerful and had assaulted her senses when he had opened his mouth and breathed in her face.

When he had grabbed her, his body had been a rancid mix of sweat, lack of personal hygiene, and putrid alcohol seeping from his pores.

Her stomach rolled as they drove down a large hill at speeds too fast for the rolling windy road. How drunk was he? Was he able to drive?

A small accident would not be the worst thing in the world, just enough to stop his truck from moving, and she hoped there were witnesses so that he could not leave the scene. But then she realized she did not have her seat belt on. She wished she could put it on, but there was no way she could accomplish that without him noticing.

Suddenly, he made a sharp right turn, causing them to fishtail and rocks to fly. Against her will, she had to reach out momentarily to catch herself. She tried to immediately resume her position, not that they were going at a much slower pace, rolling over the gravel road.

"You can give it up. I knew you were awake," he slurred. "You ain't no good as an actress. So quit pretending."

He slapped the fatty part of her butt that was up in the air because she leaned on her hip as close to the door as she could.

She quickly contemplated jumping out. He had not tied her up, most likely assuming that just knocking her senseless would probably do the trick. Her head was still a little fuzzy and, with her eyes closed, she felt like she was on a never ending circus ride that was about to make her vomit.

This was her chance, now or never. If she was going to make her get away, she had to act fast. She took a deep breath and prayed the vehicle was an older model that did not have automatic locks.

Kit reached for the door handle slowly and, in one swift motion, opened the door and hurled herself out.

ℰↄℰↄ

"You did not see where she went?" Jay screamed.

"No, by the time I came out to meet her, they were gone. I checked the elevators and the stairwell. He must have been waiting for her," Rex answered quickly.

Jay had shown up as fast as he could after Rex had called him. In the meantime, Rex had scoured the building and parking lot.

"They're pulling the tapes of the hallway now. With any luck, we can get a good picture of our kidnapper."

Kidnapper.

Kit had been kidnapped under his watch. If something happened to her, he would never forgive himself.

Sensing Rex's distress, Jay paused long enough to rest a hand on the other man's shoulder. "We will get her back. If it is the last thing we do, we're going to get her back."

Rex nodded.

"Boss," a rookie called out to Hunter.

"Yeah."

"We found this on the stairwell." With a gloved hand he held up a cell phone.

"That is Kit's," Rex confirmed miserably.

"Sarge, we also found this." He held up a small piece of paper.

Hunter looked at it and went white.

"What is it?" Rex asked.

"The final piece of the puzzle."

"Okay, men, they went this way. He must have surprised her from behind this door. Let's go. Someone send me the footage right away when we get a visual from the tape," Jay yelled as they headed down the stairs. "Rex, you're with me."

ოოო

Kit hit the ground harder than she expected, and she attempted to tuck and roll as she went. The momentum propelled her far into the ditch and her whole body hurt when she finally stopped moving. She had only a moment to collect her bearings before she knew she had to run.

She could hear the truck squeal to a stop, and she was on her feet, running wildly. She ran or hobbled as fast as she could trying to ignore the searing pain traveling through her body.

There was a patch of trees, if she could just get there, maybe she could hide.

"Kit," the man screamed.

He was chasing behind her.

"Dammit. Stop or you will pay for it, I swear."

She could hear him wheezing. She was in the woods, running for safety. Branches and leaves slapped her as she went, but she ignored them, running blindly.

"You know that there is nowhere to go. I'm going to find you."

She gasped for air but did not dare stop. She heard a branch break too close for comfort. He was closing in. She spotted a hollowed out tree covered with brush and immediately ducked inside, paying no mind to whatever animal called it home.

She was out of breath and her body ached, but she tried to make herself silent.

"I've waited too long for this, Kit, to let you go now."

Her body was trembling, and she covered her mouth with her own hand to avoid making any sound.

"Kit, I know you can hear me. You can thank your precious fiancé when you meet again for all your trouble."

She squeezed her eyes shut.

"He took me away from my family, and now it is time that I destroy his. Do you all really think I could let him get away with it? It may be hard for you all to believe, but I had a wife and kids, and he took that all away. He could not just let us be. He had to stick his nose where it didn't belong and make my wife think things that were not true. He advised her to leave me, pack up the kids, and go. When I got out of jail, I did not even know where they were.

"No one was waiting for me when I got back. Now someone else is raising my kids for me and sleeping in bed with my wife. I'll never forgive him for that. He made me alone in this world. So you have Officer Slade to blame. Two years ago, he took everything from me so a year ago I made him pay.

"When I found out you two were going to start your own family that was too much for me to take. It hardly seemed fair, after all, he put me through, but then I realized taking him out was hardly enough. He made my kids grow up without their father, and that made me full of rage. He made me out to be some sort of monster, and everybody believed it, including my family. I found joy when you lost your precious baby."

Kit held in a sob and silent tears slipped from her eyes.

"And now, Kit, I'm after you. I've done everything. I picked up, moved, and slept in my truck. I've devoted my time and all of my energy into this. Do you even care?"

He screamed as he hit a tree snapping a large stick.

The sound made her jump and crunch the leaves beneath her. Startled by her own sound, she hunkered deeper into the foliage.

"Now you have that cowboy Rex to keep you warm. Over my dead body will the widow of Officer Anderson Slade be happy. You don't deserve it." He hit another tree with a menacing crack. "You women are all the same. Just like Theresa did to me. You all up and move on at the first opportunity you get, but not this time, Kit, I am going to put an end to it today."

ↄⸯↄↄ

They sped out of town with sirens blazing.

"Do you know him?" Rex asked, anxiously clutching the door handle.

Jay's eyes were trained on the road ahead as he pushed down hard on the accelerator.

"Joseph Porter, age thirty-seven, in and out of jail for petty crimes, a known alcoholic, a real piece of work. He used to be a regular around here, drunk and disorderly, driving under the influence or while suspended. He used to beat up on his wife and terrorize his kids. She would never press any charges for fear of what he would do when he was released, until they passed the law saying if we saw any signs of abuse we could bring him in without the victim's consent. One night, he banged her up pretty good, causing her to get stitches. Andy hauled him in."

"And that is what this is all about?" Rex asked.

"Well, Andy went back out to their place and convinced Theresa, his wife, that this was no situation in which to raise kids. It must have been the straw that broke the camel's back because she moved across the country before Porter got out. He tried to raise a stink about police brutality for a while, but it never held any weight, and he's been flying under the radar ever since. We figured he must have hit rock bottom and was making himself scarce after publically embarrassing himself, but apparently he was just plotting his revenge."

"And he has kids?"

"Young ones, a boy and a girl, but as far as I know they have refused any contact with him, and he has not had the means to fight it."

"And he blames Slade."

"Apparently. I knew he was angry, but I would have never guessed all this."

"How could you? It takes a real sick bastard to pull this off."

"He must have been more sick than we gave him credit for, but it ends now," Jay said as he pushed the petal down harder.

They reached the house where Joseph Porter used to live, and Jay retrieved his gun from its holster while getting out of the car. He motioned for Rex to follow while his team surrounded the house.

The porch was sagging and creaked beneath their weight. It had been abandoned for quite some time and lack of occupancy was evident by the weeds and overgrown shrubs. The windows were broken and what glass remained was caked with dirt and debris.

Jay scanned the entrance before yelling, "Police, come out with your hands up."

After waiting a moment, he charged through the door that was barely hanging on its hinges. His gun was aimed and ready and sweat rolled down his back. Rex had his six as jay proceeded inside.

After sweeping every room, another cop yelled, "Clear. Sarge, they aren't here."

Hunter cursed in frustration.

"Where else could they be? We have to find her," Rex asked in desperation.

"I was sure they would be here."

"Sarge? We got info that Porter owns a small fishing cabin on the lake," a younger officer said breathlessly.

With a renewed spark of hope, Jay said, "What are we waiting for? Let's go."

"How far is that?" Rex asked.

"About another twelve minutes south of town," Jay said grimly as they hopped back in the squad car.

CHAPTER 24

"Come out, come out wherever you are," Joseph said in a sing song voice, swinging the branch as he went. He was close, close enough that she could smell the rancid body odor that seeped off his skin and saturated the air around him in a cloud of pungent steam, invading her nose, triggering her gag reflex.

One false move and she would be exposed. By now they would be looking for her. She needed to stay strong and wait him out until help arrived. Her shoulder ached and judging by its abnormal position she feared she had dislocated it by her descent from the truck.

She was worried about her life more than her shoulder, but she knew that, in a physical altercation, it might hinder her ability to fight back and the man had already overpowered her once.

Insects crept up her pant leg and she longed to shake them off but did not dare move an inch. Just as he was about to move farther away, a bee buzzed above her head, and she held her breath. She gently swatted, willing it to go away because she was deathly allergic.

Wouldn't that be something? If she died right here in the woods, but the cause was not because some psychopath hunted her down, but rather a simple bee sting when she was without her EPI pen.

The swatting proved to only make the bee more angry, and she squeezed her eyes shut as it came down, puncturing her arm. The prick was sharp and it stung. She jumped in reaction, causing leaves to crunch.

Oh no, this is it, she thought.

Joseph whirled around quickly and she tried to be a mannequin, knowing there would not be much time, but it was too late. She was spotted. "Got ya," he said, smiling as he yanked hard on her sore arm.

She yelped in pain and, as it seared through her body, she thought she saw stars. "No, please."

"It is too late to beg, sweetheart," he chided. "You thought you were smart, didn't you?"

Evil glinted in his deranged eyes.

"Please, listen. I got stung," she choked.

"Oh, I'm so sorry," he retorted sarcastically.

"No, you don't understand. I'm allergic. It won't be long, I'll be in shock. Do you really want me to die from a bee sting? It will take away all your satisfaction."

"You're lying," he said skeptically.

She was gasping for air and felt her throat closing up, like a golf ball was lodged in her airway. She indicated the red swelling on her arm as proof.

He looked dismayed that his plans for her might be coming to an end. "That just means, I better hurry," he grunted as he pulled a fistful of her hair. "Let's go."

Her breaths were short, and she clutched wildly at his arms as he hoisted her over his shoulder and made his way toward the dock.

He dropped her down heavily, and she groaned at the impact. Her body felt limp, and she had no strength to fight. As the seconds ticked by, she knew she was running out of time.

"This is not what I had in mind, but it will do. You're about to go swimming."

Kit's head rolled to one side as she ran out of oxygen.

"No, you do not get to pass out on me. That is way too easy."

He picked her up, placing her belly down, and grabbed her hair again. He plunged her face into the water and held it there until her brain was screaming in panic.

"This is for my time spend behind bars." He let her up, and her limbs hung at her sides. He shoved her face beneath the cold surface again. "This is for taking away my family." When he brought her back up, she was barely on the brink of consciousness, but he was not finished. "This is for thinking you could move on just like my wife, you selfish bitch."

When she came up the third time, her lips were blue and her body flopped like a ragdoll.

As he was about to push her down again he said, "This is for thinking that you and your family were better than mine."

"Stop. Police," Jay screamed with his gun pointed.

Joseph whipped around and lost his hold on Kit. She slipped beneath the surface of the cold waters.

Simultaneously, Porter reached into his pocket, and Jay pulled the trigger as Rex dove into the frigid lake.

CHAPTER 25

"If you wanted to go skinny dipping with me, you could have just said so," Rex whispered in her ear.

The monitor beeped obnoxiously in the sterile hospital room, and he squeezed Kit's cold hand.

When they had arrived on scene she had been blue and in shock. He thought she was dead, and the feeling that took over him was unlike anything he had ever felt before and something he never wished to experience again.

When the paramedics found a faint pulse, his heart had leapt with hope and joy. She had yet to wake up, and the doctors were monitoring brain activity, but he kept reminding her that she was strong and of how much she had to live for.

He called Mellie to keep her updated until she was strong enough to make the trip herself and Kit's parents were taking their time, making their way back from out of the country, but he and Andy's police family refused to leave her side.

Joseph Porter was in ICU under guard, and it made Rex's blood boil just knowing that animal was in the same building.

Jay came in after knocking softly. "How's our girl?"

"The same. They say it's a waiting game. We just wait for her to wake up."

"Okay, the detectives have some questions for you. I'll sit with her while you go."

Rex started to get up when he felt the slightest movement from Kit's hand.

He paused in anticipation. Kit moved her lips and made a gargling sound.

"Kit? Can you hear me?" Rex asked.

"How can I not?" she mumbled. "You're always talking. I would not go skinny dipping." Her eyelids fluttered open and he had never seen something so miraculous.

"Why not?" His eyes twinkled.

"Because I'm a respectable woman." Her lips curved in a small smile.

He breathed a sigh of relief. "That you are. That you are."

EPILOGUE

K it pulled onto the rocky road slowly to avoid perpetuating a cloud of dust, and she took in the smells of country living. If someone told her that she was going to miss the simplicities, she would not have believed them. She didn't think she would long to be back there, until she did.

Instead of driving all the way to her cabin, she pulled into the one across the lake. She saw him sitting on the deck, his long legs propped up with his eyes closed, the sun shining down on his rugged face.

She once again pondered the humor of surprising him by kicking over his chair and giggled to herself.

Sensing someone's presence, he opened his eyes and looked as if he saw a mirage standing right in front of him, glowing in the sunlight, her hair ablaze like fire.

The sun shone in her eyes and she could not read his facial expression underneath his squinting, but it was one fire he did not want to put out.

"Hello there, Chief," she said softly.

"What are you doing here, teach? I thought you were going to stay in Watertown?"

"I thought so too." She shrugged. "The memories

and all, but I realized it might be time for me to make some new ones."

"Is that right?" His eyes narrowed further.

"Yeah, it is. I also heard the fire department hired a full time chief. I thought I would congratulate him."

"You came all this way to congratulate me?"

"What can I say? I thought it meant more in person."

"It does," he said, standing.

"I also thought this is as good as place as any to set down some roots."

"You're moving back?"

She nodded.

"To teach?" he asked.

She shook her head. "It seems that Andy left me his life insurance. He had it changed after he found out about the baby. I thought I would take the time to write, like I always wanted. Besides, I have been told I have a heck of a story."

"That you do. Well, I suppose congratulations are in order to you as well."

"Thank you."

They fell into silence.

"I wish you all the luck in telling your story."

She bit her lip.

"Rex, I was hoping to make many more stories here. I lost someone that I loved."

"Yes," he answered.

"And he would have wanted me to be happy."

"What about what you want? Is there room for more than one love of your life?"

She met his eye. "Yes," she said slowly. "There is."

"Do I know him?" he asked, moving closer.

"I think so. First impression, he is a real ass, but once you get to know him, he's kind, genuine, and respectable."

"You forgot irresistibly handsome."

She laughed. "How could I forget?"

He cupped her face in his hands, and she wrapped her arms around his waist.

"Are you ready to move on? Because I'm a selfish man. I want all of you."

"You have all of me, and I'm ready to move on, here with you," she whispered.

"I never knew what I was missing until I found you," he said gruffly.

"Well technically, I found you. I'm the one that moved here," she said, smiling.

His mouth twitched. "Have I ever mentioned you're incredibly irritating?"

"You may have mentioned that once or twice."

He smiled before his mouth crushed down on hers passionately.

When they finally came up for air, he nibbled her ear. "What can I do for you?"

"First things first. I'm parched and have been craving some iced tea."

"Sweet or unsweet?" he asked, nuzzling her neck.

"Sweet, of course. I want all the Southern comforts."

About the Author

Jen Midkiff, also known as JD Davis, is from a midwestern town where she works as a hairstylist. She is a devoted wife and mother to triplet preschool aged boys. When she isn't running half marathons, managing her salon, or taking care of her family, she enjoys writing in her spare time. *Southern Comfort* is her third published novel and she has more mystery/romance novels that will be coming out in the future. Be on the lookout for her upcoming titles.